"I think you're the one who's amazing."

Cora blinked. Where had that come from? "What?" she asked.

"You stepped in front of Rain to protect that boy from my dog," Tripp explained.

"I didn't—"

He placed a hand on her arm and squeezed. "You shifted yourself to stand in front of Rain and me and were ready to defend."

She looked from Tripp to the spot where she stood a few minutes ago and replayed the scene in her head. A smile broke out over her face, one she knew probably looked goofy and proud.

"I did," she whispered.

"You did. You're the bravest person I know," he whispered back. He stepped closer, took a lock of her hair and folded it around her ear, exposing her scars. Her nerves skittered the way they always did when her scars were out in the open. But maybe they also skittered because of Tripp's touch.

What was it about this man? This man who saw her and didn't shy away?

Despite the frigid temperature, warmth spread through her chest.

Elizabeth Long writes romance full of heart and laced with humor. Rainy days and comfy sweatpants are her ideal working conditions, and she usually depletes her e-reader's battery before her cell phone's. Elizabeth prefers the mountains to beaches, but will travel anywhere with her family as long as they return home to Texas. She only wishes the Lone Star State's weather would allow her to wear more sweaters. You can find Elizabeth at elizabethlongbooks.com.

Books by Elizabeth Long

Love Inspired

Snowbound with Her Protector

Visit the Author Profile page at LoveInspired.com.

Then shall we know, if we follow on to know the Lord: his going forth is prepared as the morning; and he shall come unto us as the rain, as the latter and former rain unto the earth.
—*Hosea* 6:3

For Rachele Bland,

Crysta Crum,

Daniel Mills,

Kathleen Nile,

Sally Pearce,

Sean Sell,

Chris Thelen,

Charlotte Thompson, and

Bonnie Welday.

Because you, also, once helped someone with his heart.

Chapter One

Tripp Blackburn had never seen a parade of pregnant women. While he stood sentry and held the door of the Elk Run Diner, a line of women with all sizes of baby bumps walked through. For a small Wyoming ranch town, these must be frighteningly fertile fields.

Probably a good thing he was just visiting from Colorado.

He didn't know much about pregnant women. Between his previous military service and his current career as a therapy and service-dog trainer, he wasn't around expectant mothers too often. But he offered this group a wide smile and tipped his Stetson to a few.

The final woman, petite with a brown bob that hid part of her face, walked through. Clutching a black backpack against her chest, she murmured, "Thank you."

He gave her his best smile. "So when's the big day?" he asked as he followed her into the restaurant.

Without taking her eyes off the group, she said in a flat tone, "I'm not pregnant."

Tripp's boot stumbled on the checkered linoleum, and he almost took a nosedive. He deserved to be put in the doghouse for his insensitive comment and would happily crawl there if he knew where one was located.

"I apologize. I thought—"

"Careful," she said with an edge to her low, husky voice, her watchful gaze glued to the women seating themselves at a line of square tables. "If you keep going with what you thought about my appearance and how I do or don't look pregnant, it might go poorly for you."

If he could find scraps of driftwood, he'd go make that doghouse and then crawl right into it. But he didn't think he could find any in the foothills of the mountains in Elk Run, Wyoming.

"I apologize." He cleared his throat. "Maybe we could start over?"

Her eyes darted back to the women. As she perused the crew, worry drew over her face. "I have to get back to my group."

With a curt nod to him, she strode to the women.

He ran a hand through his hair. It was time to get a haircut. And find some new social skills. His first interaction in a new town couldn't have gone worse if he'd tried.

Still. Something about the woman made him take a closer look.

She crouched low to murmur to one, offered an encouraging squeeze to others, wiped tears off the cheek of another. She was was their protector. Their confidante. Their warrior wrapped up in the package of a five-foot-two-inch spitfire with daring eyes and a soft touch.

A heavy clap on his shoulder jolted him out of his thoughts. "Tripp?"

He turned and saw the face of his friend.

The years since he'd served in the army had etched lines in the sides of Chase Cross's eyes. The cowboy looked good. Healthy. Happy.

"It's been a long time," Tripp said as they shook hands.

Chase stepped back to reveal a second man. His mirror image. "This is my twin brother, Hunter."

Hunter shook Tripp's hand and nodded. "Good to meet you."

Hunter sat in a booth that faced the rest of the patrons of the restaurant, and Tripp slid in next to him.

Chase placed himself opposite them, his back to the room, and said with a chagrined smile, "We find that when we sit side by side across from people, it freaks them out a little."

"You don't want to have to stare at our ugly mugs," Hunter murmured.

"You guys can't be that bad-looking. Someone married Chase," Tripp said to his friend. "But seriously. Congratulations to you. It was good to hear you found someone. When's she due?"

"Two weeks now."

A waitress sidled up to their table, her name tag indicating they should call her Stacy. A pencil stuck out of her greying blonde hair. It was styled like a football helmet. "What can I get for you boys today?"

"We'll have the Partridge in a Pear Tree and a pot of coffee," Chase said.

One drawn-in eyebrow quirked on her face. "You think you can tackle it this time?"

He nodded his head to Tripp. "We've got one more this round. And this man knows how to eat."

"You can do it. I believe in you, hon," Stacy said as she turned to leave.

"What did we just order?" Tripp asked.

"Basically every breakfast item on the menu. Twelve delicious items," Chase said. "If we finish the platter, we get a free dessert. Which we won't need because if we finish, they'll have to roll us out of here in a wheelbarrow. The town demanded they serve it year-round even though it's got a Christmas theme."

Tripp placed a hand over his stomach and pledged, "I'll do my best."

The waitress brought a carafe of coffee to their table and poured their mugs.

"The last time I saw you was on base overseas, what… four years ago?" Chase asked. "As I recall, I was waving to you and your dog from a chopper."

A lump formed in Tripp's throat. "We lost Storm not long after that."

Chase lowered his voice. "I hadn't heard. Sorry, man."

It took a long time for Tripp's unit to recover after the loss of the Labrador retriever. The loyal canine had used his gifts to sniff out explosives, but had also served in an unofficial capacity as a combat-stress control dog. Tripp had never seen a dog so diversely wired for battle and for empathy.

"When I separated from the military, I returned to the mainland and tracked down Storm's breeders. I've got his grand-dog. Rain. She helps me out in an official support capacity." Tripp needed a service dog due to issues with his heart and now helped others find that same gift for themselves.

Chase glanced around the diner. "She here?"

"Left her at the ranch. I wasn't quite sure what to expect in town." Even though service dogs had a legal and necessary place in public spaces, he tried to be sensitive to those around him when he could. "Plus, she needed some freedom after our long car ride."

His friend eyed him. "You okay without her?"

"Yeah. Thanks."

The waitress plunked down their breakfast platter. Steam wafted off the sausages, bacon, and grits. The stack of thick, fluffy pancakes stood eight deep, only slightly higher than the piles of waffles and toast. *Feast* seemed too small a word to describe the display in the middle of the table.

His mouth watered. Finishing the Partridge was going to be fun.

"How long are you in town?" Chase asked as he piled food on his plate.

"Five days."

Four Cross Ranch was a fully functioning cattle ranch that included a lodge and individual cabins used in a non-profit capacity designed to support military families. Tripp was slated to work with one of the families.

He unrolled his silverware from the paper napkin. "I'll work at your ranch with the veteran's son over the next few days. We're supposed to meet later today to get acquainted."

"He's a cute little boy from a good family."

"I'm glad your organization is able to help them." He picked up his fork. "I've also got a half sister who lives in the area, and I'll spend some time with her while I'm here."

If she'd let him. All he had to show for her was an email he received three months ago saying she'd moved from Colorado to Wyoming. No idea why. No response to his reply.

With no answers, he focused on consuming an obscene amount of breakfast food while listening to the Cross brothers.

Cora Cross was going to have to talk to him. The idiot who thought she was pregnant was sitting with her brothers. There was just no way to avoid him.

She needed her brothers' help. Now.

After saying goodbye to her girls, she hiked her backpack over one of her shoulders and headed to their table.

Upon her arrival, she announced, "Your friend here needs to learn to resist asking strangers if they're pregnant."

Chase coughed as if he had inhaled his drink down the wrong pipe. Hunter turned and silently glared at the stranger.

A hint of red hit the man's face along with an embarrassed smile. Shifting his attention to her brothers, he explained, "Several pregnant women walked into the restaurant with her. It was clear they were in a group. I didn't take a good look at her." He turned his eyes to Cora. "I didn't take a good look at you."

With his face pinched in disapproval, Hunter said in an incredulous tone, "She's the most sought-after midwife in the state of Wyoming. She holds a brunch here every Saturday for expectant mothers from surrounding counties."

Muscles in the man's square jaw clenched.

He had dusty-colored hair, not too blond and not too brown. It was of a longer length—not shaggy, but not a close cut. His eyes were a blue hue—not dark, but also not light. Just beautiful. Intriguing.

"I'm Cora. Cora Cross."

The man extended his hand to shake hers, a glint in his eye. "Tripp Blackburn," he said. His grip was warm, rough, and a little bit daring.

"Tripp's going to work with one of the families at the ranch this week." Chase picked up his coffee. "Did you come over because you want to help with our Partridge in a Pear Tree?"

She laughed. "Not on your life. I was enjoying my salad,

thank you very much. Something you guys could stand to eat once in a while."

"Too healthy," Hunter grunted just before he shoveled a bite of sausage and pancake drenched in syrup into his mouth.

Chase chuckled and asked, "There something we can do for you, Cora?"

She looked at the three men. She didn't want to have to do this in front of a stranger.

But a pregnant woman in need trumped her pride. Every time.

Clearing her throat, she lifted her chin. "I need to go down to the Klines."

Thunder crossed Hunter's face. The Klines's ornery reputation spanned four generations and three counties. "Why?" he growled.

"Sally's pregnant again. Someone saw her at the farmer's market this morning. Said she didn't look good." She tamped down the years-long embarrassment. "I, um… I need help with—"

"The guard dogs," Hunter said, finishing her sentence. They locked eyes, and the memory of *that day* seemed to pass between them.

"Guard dogs?" Tripp asked, his entire posture on alert, his blue eyes fierce and laced with concern.

No way was Cora going to explain the situation to a complete stranger. Ignoring him, she shot her gaze from one brother to the other.

"I can't go with you," Hunter said. "The vet's coming to the ranch in half an hour, and I need to be there."

She shifted her focus to Chase and raised her eyebrows in question to her other brother.

"I'm sorry, Cora," Chase said with regret in his voice. "Lexi and I are headed to the doctor right after this."

"Everything okay?"

Chase nodded. "Regular checkup."

She could feel Tripp's stare on her.

No way did she want to ask for help from a stranger. Cora looked down, sighed, then locked eyes with Tripp. "How do you feel about dogs?"

A smile tugged at his lips. "I like dogs."

"You won't like these dogs." She fidgeted with the thick strap of her backpack. "Do you have time to come with me on an errand?"

"I can vouch for him," Chase said good-naturedly. "He certainly watched my back a couple of times over the years."

Heat hit her face as she waited for Tripp's reply.

He nodded to her. "I'm in town for the next five days and I'd be happy to help in any way I can while I'm here."

Oh. Cora breathed out her relief.

This was a win-win. Cora would go to the Klines's with the man from out of town who would protect her from the dogs, not knowing anything about why they put the fear of God into her, and then he'd leave town and everything would go back to normal. She could tuck her shame back inside her pocket, and her brothers would be there to take her to the Klines's place if the need arose again.

"That would be kind of you. Thank you," she said.

"Just keep her safe. Distract Jekyll and Hyde. And," Hunter murmured, "you might want to avoid the county line."

Tripp cocked his head. "Why's that?"

"Cora's got a heavy foot."

She darted a glare to her brother.

"Something to know about Tripp—" Chase began.

Cora held up her hand. "I need to get to Sally." She didn't have time to know anything about Tripp, which was just as well. She looked at him. "You ready to go?"

"I'll have to help you two tackle the Partridge another time," Tripp said to Hunter and Chase before he swiped his napkin across his mouth and pushed out of his seat. "We'll get it done before I leave town."

Hunter gave him a nod of respect.

"Do you need to get Rain?" Chase asked Tripp, concern in his voice.

"It's all good," Tripp said. "Thanks."

Cora didn't notice a wedding band. Rain must be his girlfriend.

Why did that feel disappointing?

While she unclipped her car keys from the carabiner on her backpack, she mulled over the name. *Rayne. Rainn. Raine.* Tripp Blackburn and his handsome looks probably meant she was beautiful. The kind of woman with no scars inside or out. The kind of woman who was unlike Cora. On all counts.

Cora drew her hand across her long bangs, making sure her scars were hidden safely behind her hair.

Tripp slid out of the booth and looked to her. "You ready to throw me to the Klines?"

"No. I'm ready to throw you to the dogs."

Tripp stared out the passenger window of Cora's massive black SUV and figured it was perfect that after mistakenly asking Cora if she was pregnant that she would throw him to the dogs. He also wondered why a woman so small owned the equivalent of a battle cruiser of a car.

"I was going to offer to drive—"

"Thanks," she said, adjusting the mirror, "but I drive these parts all the time. Not many midwives around here, so I know all the shortcuts."

A fiery glint filled her eyes as she cranked up the vehicle.

She ripped off the top of a water bottle and downed the entirety of its contents. With no regard for his personal space, she leaned across him and tore open the glove compartment, hauled out a giant package of Twizzlers, and slammed the small storage space closed.

Her focus was unparalleled. He wasn't even sure she remembered he was in the car.

What was going on with this woman?

Should he be scared?

She put the vehicle in Reverse and backed out of her space, then shifted into Drive. Gravel crushed under the huge tires and pinged against the hub caps as she sped out of the parking lot and hung a right onto the paved road.

This must be the heavy foot that Hunter had referred to. What had Tripp gotten himself into?

"Uh…" He didn't know where to start. "I think there's a speed trap up here. You might want to be careful."

He had no idea if there was a speed trap or not. He just needed to think of some way to slow her down.

"Don't worry. Sherriff Langston and I have an understanding. I only speed when a baby needs me."

He gripped the grab handle at his head. "Is that why you have to be careful of the county line?"

"Yes. Other officers aren't quite as understanding," she said, her eyes wild, taking in her surroundings. "Then again, I haven't delivered their grandbabies."

She hit a long stretch of road and, terrifyingly, put her

knees in control of the steering wheel while she ripped open the package of licorice.

With the candy between her legs and one hand now on the steering wheel, she punched at the radio controls. She chose a playlist called "Pre" and unapologetically turned the volume to a startling volume. An 80s girl band started harmonizing that they couldn't stop the world.

She was in a zone. Preparing for whatever might lie ahead.

If Tripp wasn't so fascinated, he'd be fearing for his life.

After snagging two long pieces of licorice, she shoved the ends into her mouth and began chewing. There was nothing attractive about it and somehow everything about it was attractive.

She had completely transformed.

Who was this tiny, husky-voiced, warrior who drove like a rocket, ate Twizzlers before battle, and was hurling them down the road into oblivion?

The song came to a halt and a blessed quiet descended over the car for two-point-five seconds before the rapid notes of a bass guitar opened for the next song. The buildup led to a louder note that had Cora slamming the heel of her hand in time with the forceful sounds of the electric guitar. Tripp's memory flashed to the movie attached to the song. An underdog boxer.

She slowed for a curve in the road, speeding up when she saw no one was coming in the opposite direction.

Did she want him to strategically lean his weight into the turn? He decided not to ask in case the answer was yes.

Again, he wondered who this woman was. And again, he wondered if he'd live long enough to find out.

The music switched one more time, this song from

the 70s advising him, wisely he thought, to roll with the changes.

He leaned back in his chair, angled his hat over his brow, and closed his eyes. If she flung them to their death, it might be best not to know it was coming.

A few minutes later, the music ended and Cora braked to a tight stop, leaving an alarming silence that caused him to sit up straight.

Tripp caught his breath while he took in the beat-up gate and desolate property before him. A ramshackle house was perched precariously twenty yards away, nothing but dirt and a dilapidated swing set outside the homestead. Empty land rolled out for miles behind the property.

"What's the plan?" Tripp asked, studying the tall, unkempt bushes and trees along the fence line.

"They know we're here. Ethan Kline will show up with a shotgun on the porch. It's his daughter, Sally, who I'm coming to see. His son, Samuel, will come out from around the back to show support."

"Also with a shotgun?" Tripp peered closer at the house. Did a curtain in the window just move?

He didn't like this.

"Yes. But they're harmless," she said.

"In my experience, firearms are never harmless."

"If Sally's husband is home, he'll make them let me in. If he's not home, she'll do it. But at some point, Samuel will unleash the dogs. And that's where things could get tricky."

Dogs, he could handle. "Why does it get—"

Out of the house bounded two giant animals, both an intimidating mix of rottweiler and pit bull, with slobbery, caustic barks.

A sheen of dust covered their sleek black coats. Intriguing brown patches were above their eyes, on their muzzles, and undersides. The alpha dog weighed at least a hundred and ten pounds. Cora's formidable internal strength was wrapped in a petite body that would get mowed over by those canines.

After one breath, Tripp said in a firm voice, "I've got this."

She didn't answer him.

When he turned to her, he didn't expect to see such distinct fear behind the warrior princess's eyes. "Cora?"

Cora's memory flashed to the pack of wolves. When she was seventeen. When she was unsafe.

"Cora."

Her head jerked back to present day at the sound of her name. She looked at Tripp. His eyes held concern. And strength. How many times had he called her name before she heard him?

While inhaling one long calming pull of air, she schooled her features to mask the emotion she must have shown. This was not the time for her to fall apart. She'd do that later, when she was alone. Like she always did.

After clearing her throat, she tightened her voice. "You've got this?"

"Yes," he said, studying her face. "Do you know their names?"

"Jekyll and Hyde. Jekyll is the bigger one."

"The alpha. Okay, let's move."

Cora opened her door and hopped down from the vehicle. She slid her backpack over both shoulders and secured the straps. Tightly.

Her entire body froze in place. Her feet rooted themselves to the ground, begging her to stay put.

No, no, no, no, no.

She wasn't going to freeze. Not now. Not in front of people.

She wanted to trust Tripp. But she needed more than anything to trust God to take care of her. And that wasn't something she ever imagined she would be able to do.

With three fingers, she traced the scars that ran from her scalp, down her temple and faded at her cheekbone.

Did they mean that God hadn't taken care of her when she was seventeen? Or were the scars evidence of His vast protection?

What would it be like if Cora could live like she believed the latter?

She inhaled deeply, demanding her body to move. A pregnant momma was in need. She couldn't be panicked. She'd already released all her stress with the Twizzlers and the music on the way here just like she always did.

She had to leave any bit of pressure behind, because when she entered the realm of midwifery, she was the calm in that storm.

Engaging every muscle in her body, she dragged her feet out of the concrete of fear and slid around her SUV toward the horrendous barks.

But her heart felt like it stopped when she rounded the car.

Where was Tripp?

Her breathing became shallow.

Where was Tripp?

Where was Grant?

No. Not Grant.

Grant had abandoned her to the wolves when she was seventeen.

Where was Tripp?

The next breath felt like like oxygen was being dragged through sludge into her body.

The barking. The lack of breath. The darkness of abandonment—it all caved in on her.

"Cora!" Tripp yelled from somewhere.

She drew in another shallow breath, turned her head to follow the sound of her name, and saw that the barking dogs, baring their teeth, were also headed in that direction. Away from her.

Down the fence line, Tripp waited for the canines.

His demeanor calm, posture relaxed, he spoke words she couldn't hear while he flipped small pieces of something from his pocket several feet in front of him. Every so often, he'd take two relaxed steps backward.

The dogs became distracted and gobbled up the bites of whatever Tripp was leaving on the ground.

A trail of treats leading *away* from her.

Something in her chest squeezed. He was leading them away from her. Putting himself at risk. And he didn't appear scared in the slightest.

In fact, he seemed in his element. Calm. Solid. Murmuring gentle words to the dogs, not making eye contact with her or with them, casually flipping bits to the ground.

Quickly, she unlatched the gate and hurried in the direction of the house.

"Slowly, Cora," Tripp called without looking at her, his voice still gentle.

Slowly. That made sense.

Because the massive barking dogs with fangs and claws might believe she was running away from them. Which she *was*, because that seemed the most logical course of action.

But apparently, Tripp thought it was best to walk. She'd have to discuss it with him later.

For now, she tamped down her nerves. And she walked.

Per usual, Ethan Kline had showed up on the porch,

shotgun in hand. The five-o'clock shadow was close to beard status, and his overalls bulged at his belly.

Samuel showed up, just as she predicted, his grimy scowl matching his father's.

When she reached the porch's rotting wood, Ethan turned his head and spat on the dusty floor. "I see you brought a dog whisperer today. This your way of getting to Sally?"

She swallowed down her anxiety and controlled her voice to sound relaxed. "How are you today, Mr. Kline?"

He grunted. "I know why you're here, and we're not interested in your help."

"Daddy, stop giving Cora a hard time," a voice called from inside. Sally shoved open the screen door and stood beside her father. "Morning, Cora. I see your girls couldn't keep their mouths shut."

The woman's blunt words were only for show. Standing five foot ten with broad shoulders and a solid figure, Sally was almost as intimidating as the men in her family, save the hint of vulnerability in her eyes.

Cora placed one foot on a higher step, a show to suggest she was a casual friend. "Could we talk in private?"

After an exam and brief consultation with Sally, Cora offered a quick goodbye. She hit the bottom of the porch steps and started to jog in the direction of her SUV, then stopped when she didn't hear the familiar jingle on her carabiner.

Had she forgotten her keys in the Kline house?

She slung her backpack off her back and saw the keys were in their usual place, just caught on some loose stitching.

Her fingers moved to jostle them free but froze at the sound of the barking.

Panic coursed through her veins, and her feet felt like they were stapled to the ground.

Yelling registered, but she could only stare in horror as a massive dog bounded toward her with his sharp teeth bared.

Where was Tripp?

More yelling. More barking. More gasps for breath.

Samuel held one of the dogs back, but looked like he was losing the battle.

"Throw your backpack, Cora."

Her name. Her name grounded her. She understood.

She hurled her backpack to the side of the incoming canine's head, providing a distraction.

Tripp bounded in front of her, using his body to block her from the rottweiler. "Get to the car," he said, his breaths heavy, but his voice calm.

With the preoccupied dog tearing into her backpack, she ran to the wooden fence. She didn't want to stop and deal with the gate, and, like any girl who grew up on a ranch, launched herself off the first rung and hopped over the fence.

Only she landed in a leaf-covered ditch, miscalculating her footing. Her right ankle wrenched at an unnatural angle, and pain seared up the outside of her calf.

She gritted her teeth and held on to the cry in her throat.

Tripp kneeled and talked calmly to whom she now recognized as Hyde, then stood, threw her torn backpack over one of his shoulders, and walked toward her. Hyde stayed where he was. After five steps, Tripp turned back to the dog, praised him, and threw him something from his pocket. Hyde caught the treat, chomped it down, and wagged his tail as if waving goodbye.

As if he hadn't just almost attacked Cora.

Tripp continued through the gate to her, his piercing blue eyes holding her in place. "You okay?"

She nodded once.

"I'm driving," he declared, releasing the keys from the carabiner, then returning her war-torn backpack to her. The front pocket hung by a few stitches, the fabric's thick canvas edges jagged.

He hit Unlock on her key fob and went to open her door for her.

"I've got it," she said. He nodded and walked around the car.

She felt it coming. Her post-appointment release.

The tsunami of emotions didn't care that a dog had awakened an old trauma, that she was with a practical stranger, or that she had injured herself in the fall. The feelings were going to flood out of her whether she was ready or not.

Tripp turned to her and asked softly, "Cora, what happened back there?"

She closed her eyes and took a breath. The pressure mounted in her chest. "I need you to do me three favors, Tripp Blackburn."

"O-o-o-kay," he said, drawing out the word with a tentative tone.

"First, I need you to turn on the playlist called 'Post' and leave it at volume level eight. Please." She sucked in a shaky breath. The dam was going to break. "Second, I need you to face forward and ignore me on the drive. Just know that this is normal for me. It's healthy. A release."

"What's a re—"

"Please." Her voice shook. "Now."

"Okay, Cora," he said gently. "What's the third thing?"

"I'll tell you when we're closer to town."

She heard him hit a few buttons. The first few notes of a soothing piano melody filled the car as he threw the SUV into Drive and maneuvered the turn-around leading off the Kline property.

Away from the pressure.

Away from the burden.

Just away.

And as the soft notes of the song floated to her, enveloping her in their comfort, tears streamed down her face, carrying with them the responsibility of helping a woman and her child. The strain. The fears. The stress. All swept away by her tears.

Like they always were.

The heaviness in her chest began to lift.

Each song that played gave her more release, returned her breath, and filled her lungs with oxygen.

The last of her tears slowly dripped off her jawline. Tripp curled a handkerchief into her hand. Still with her eyes closed, she wiped her face with the soft cloth.

A few more moments passed.

"Cora?"

She cleared the last of the emotion from her throat and took one last cleansing breath. "Yes."

"What's going on?"

She opened her eyes and, leaving her head resting against the headrest, turned her neck to look at Tripp. Concern lined his face, just like it had his voice.

"I asked you to ignore me, and you agreed."

"All due respect, but I wasn't raised to ignore someone who's crying."

The road wound around a hill, and Cora noticed how calming Tripp's driving was. "I'm letting you off the hook," she said.

"Does that mean I don't have to do your third favor?"

"Oh, no." The emotional release felt good. But instead of feeling total relief, there was the physical pain in her ankle. "I definitely need you to do me that favor."

He turned his head and glanced at her. "And what would that be?"

"I need you to drop me off at the hospital."

"Sure. Are you meeting a patient there?"

"No," she said, shifting in her seat, the movement causing her to grimace in pain. "I think I broke my ankle when I hopped that fence."

Chapter Two

"Four weeks?" Cora tried her best not to yell at Dr. Evans, but she knew she'd raised her voice.

"Yes," the doctor said.

She shook her head, grappling with the news. "Four weeks?"

Dr. Evans wore the same peaceful smile Cora had always known the woman to have on the ER floor. Not a stitch of makeup, bifocals around her neck, and a piece of paper folded in her hand, she said, "I knew you'd be trouble as a patient." She turned to Tripp. "Brilliant midwife, though."

Tripp looked to her with concern, but there was a touch of admiration in his voice when he murmured, "I can see how that might be the case."

The man refused to leave, then informed her in what she guessed was his best military authority voice that he would be staying for the doctor's report under the orders of her brothers.

She knew which battles to pick with her brothers and told Dr. Evans she could speak freely.

Still, having the handsome—and now brooding—Tripp Blackburn in her hospital room while she found out her world was about to change was not her favorite.

She stared at her injured ankle, which was wrapped in an ice pack and propped on hospital pillows.

"The MRI shows one of your lateral ligaments is torn," the doctor said, repeating the diagnosis she'd begun the conversation with. The one where she also mentioned being in a medical boot for four weeks.

The word hit her in the stomach and soured. "Torn?" Cora knew she was in pain, but torn? A torn ligament.

"Yes. The good news is it's not a big tear. It looks like you have a good chance to heal well. You'll wear a medical boot for four weeks, but only be on crutches for two of those. I don't feel like I need to refer you to an orthopedist unless you want to go that route, but I have an excellent physical therapist I want you to see once you get out of the boot."

Normallly, she only saw Dr. Evans when she brought in one of her expectant mommas. She considered the woman a trusted friend of sorts. But the doctor's orders sent stress down her spine.

An orthopedist would require a longer drive, more cost, and more time. She'd take the small-town-doctor treatment any day of the week.

Dr. Evans handed her the piece of paper. Printed at the top was the name of the physical therapist and a phone number. Cora recognized the name. A girl from high-school days, a wallflower with a painful crush on her younger brother, Ryder. But she couldn't focus on that now.

"At the one-month mark, we'll reevaluate. If everything has healed well, we'll get you out of that boot."

Cora understood how Dr. Evans handled patients. She gave them the news quickly, then waited for the patient to react. Only Cora had no clue how to respond. "I can't wear a boot for four weeks," she blurted.

"I'm not saying this is going to be easy for you," the doctor said, "but the more you can rest it, the better. Take your anti-inflammatories and keep it elevated as much as possible, especially in the beginning."

She stared, unmoving. The words hit her like molasses, slowly covering her in the sticky reality of her injury.

"Cora?" Tripp ran the back of his hand down Cora's arm.

She jolted and looked to him. "Babies don't care about boots."

"What?" he asked, searching her face.

"Babies don't care about torn ligaments or boots and they won't wait four weeks." She returned her focus to the doctor, trying to tamp down the panic that was rising in her throat. "That's my driving foot."

"I don't think it's safe for you to drive," Tripp said. He cleared his throat. "And I definitely don't think it's safe for you to drive with a boot on your foot."

"Dr. Evans," she implored, "as you well know, I deliver babies. I don't know if I can properly do my job wearing a boot."

The doctor crossed her arms. Not a good sign. "How many of your patients are due in the next two weeks?"

"You know it doesn't work like that. Some come early."

"Okay. How many are due in the next month?"

She blew out a breath and mentally counted. "Maybe four."

"Four. So you have four possible births, and all the appointments that get more regular as the due date approaches."

"Yes."

"As far as exams and deliveries go, you'll find your equilibrium with the boot. It might involve the use of a chair."

"But—"

"You'll figure it out, Cora," Dr. Evans said, sprinkling compassion and encouragement into her hard truths about the boot, the way Cora had seen her talk to other patients.

She released a long, resigned sign. "Thank you," she muttered.

"You don't have to thank me. I just know it's true. You'll figure it out, and as far as driving goes—"

"I've got her," Tripp said, and both women turned their heads to him. He nodded, his face serious. "I've got her. I'll drive her wherever she needs to go."

"You can't do that," Cora said.

"It's my fault this happened, so I'll be the one driving you around. And if you need additional help, let me know."

The idea bounced around her head. There was no denying she was going to need help. She could probably handle a few days with Tripp Blackburn at the wheel. "Thank you. I'll take you up on that and then figure out what to do after five days. Maybe my brothers will be able to help after you leave town."

Except Chase and Lexi's baby was due soon. That'd put a wrinkle in this plan.

"Not necessary," Tripp said.

She looked to him, confused.

The doctor interjected, "I want to be clear. Five days in the boot won't be enough."

Trip nodded and locked his eyes onto Cora's. "I've got a business at home that slows during winter. You need someone with a flexible schedule who can help you. I'm staying for four weeks."

She almost fell out of her hospital bed. "What? Why would you do that?"

His eyes darkened, and took on a serious tone. "Because this is my fault."

"It's not your fault."

"It is," he said as he turned to the windows, pulled out his phone, and began furiously tapping the screen.

Dr. Evans clapped once gently to turn the attention to her. "My work is done here. I'll get your discharge papers started. DeeDee is out sick today, so the process is slower than its normal slow. Settle in for a little while and we'll get you out of here as fast as we can. Do you want an anti-inflammatory while you wait?"

Her throbbing ankle voted yes, and Cora nodded.

"And for the record—" Dr. Evans leaned in "—I like him."

Cora frowned, which only made the doctor laugh.

As Dr. Evans left the room, a young woman entered.

"Cora?" Haley Seddington asked as she stood just inside the door. "I drove by earlier and saw someone walking you in, but I couldn't get back here any earlier to check on you. Are you okay?"

"I'm fine," Cora said in a calming voice. "Just my ankle."

"I'm sorry I wasn't there—"

Tripp turned around. "Haley?"

The girl's words skidded to a stop. At the sight of Tripp, her eyes grew wide with recognition, shock, and no small amount of fear.

Before Cora knew what was happening, Tripp had engulfed Haley into his arms. "Hay-Bear," he whispered into her hair.

With her face pressed to Tripp's chest and turned in Cora's direction, Haley shook her head quickly a few times at Cora, a look of desperation in her eyes.

Tripp released Haley from the embrace, but held her in front of him.

"I—I… What are you doing here?" Haley asked.

"I'm here on business. Just got here today and was going to call you." He kept her under his arm as he turned her to Cora. "Cora, this is my baby sister."

"Half sister," Haley said with a slight wobble in her voice.

Tension choked the air between the three of them. How Tripp couldn't feel Haley's stiffness in his arms was beyond Cora. But she couldn't solve that right now. This very second, Cora had to decide how to play the situation in front of her. She went with honesty.

"I didn't realize she had a half brother." However, it made sense. Two sets of crystal-blue eyes stared back at her. One set full of pride. The other terrified.

"How do you guys know each other?" Tripp looked from Cora to Haley, his gaze settling on his sister.

"Church," Haley said quietly. "I met her at church."

"That's good," Tripp said to her, then he shifted his focus to Cora. "That's really good."

Something thick was behind his words. Cora had a guess. She'd met Haley in church at a very low point for the girl. She wondered if Tripp knew the turnaround Haley had made in her life. But it was becoming more and more clear that Tripp didn't know everything about his half sister.

"What are *you* doing here?" Haley asked Tripp.

"I came to town for a job. Wanted to surprise you. Which it looks like I did." He studied her face. "I'd love to catch up while I'm here."

"Oh." The girl's face flushed. "Oh. Well, um, I'm pretty busy the next few days. I don't know exactly—"

"That's okay," he said. "I'll be here for the next four weeks."

"Four weeks?" Haley's shock sounded like Cora felt, but for completely different reasons. She shot a look to Cora, then cleared her throat. "Cora, is there anything I can help you with?"

"Not right now, thank you," she said, trying to give Haley the exit she thought the girl wanted.

Tripp kissed Haley on the side of the head. "We'll catch up later."

They said their goodbyes, then Haley scurried out of the room, and silence stretched out while Tripp frowned at the door.

Each moment allowed Cora to put together the pieces of the scene that had just taken place in front of her. Each moment weighed heavily on her heart.

And each moment confirmed that the girl who'd just walked out of the room was Tripp's unmarried, nineteen-year-old half sister.

The newest member of Cora's pregnancy group.

Something was wrong with Haley, but Tripp hadn't been around his half sister enough to know what exactly was going on. Just something in his gut. And maybe her weird reaction to seeing him.

Even though his heart was fine today, he wished Rain was with him. Somehow, he thought she could help him with Haley.

But this was the least of Tripp's worries as Chase and Hunter stormed through the door of Cora's hospital room and beelined it to her bed to engulf her in hugs.

"I'm okay, you guys. It's just my ankle," she told them as they shot questions at her.

Chase looked at him. "Could we speak to you outside, please?"

"Absolutely," he said in a neutral tone.

"You guys," Cora groaned.

"We're just going to have a talk," Hunter said.

"It was not Tripp's fault," she called to them.

Tripp glanced to Cora in time to see her roll her eyes, then he walked through the door Hunter held open and followed them to the small waiting room.

He knew that Cora's brothers were going to kill him. But only if they could get to him before he wrung their sister's neck.

He shoved a hand through his hair. What was she thinking? How could she have not told him she was injured?

But there was more.

If he replayed her reactions from the moment they'd driven onto the Kline property, he knew he had missed something. Big.

He felt like an idiot. An idiot with a lot of questions for a pint-size warrior with pretty hazel eyes.

But first, he had to deal with the Cross brothers, who stood, wide stances and arms crossed, glaring at him with matching looks of thunder.

"What in the world happened?" Chase growled.

"She wrenched her ankle after hopping a fence."

"Why would she have hopped a fence?"

"She was running away from one of the dogs."

Chase shook his head in confusion. "How could that have happened?"

Tripp saw the concern in their eyes and sympathized. He knocked his intensity down a few notches and quieted his voice. "I'd like to ask you the same thing."

Instead of joining Chase and laying into Tripp, Hunter

remained quiet, watching with intention. Which is why Tripp homed in on him. "Here's what I know. You told me about Jekyll and Hyde, aptly named, I might add, and you asked me to distract them so Cora could get to the house."

"I asked you to keep her safe," Hunter said slowly.

"And how am I supposed to do that if I don't have all the information?" Tripp leaned closer. "She flat-out panicked with those dogs. It was almost as if she was having some sort of PTSD reaction."

Chase and Hunter exchanged a look.

Hunter's face shuttered closed. He crossed his arms over his puffed-up chest and finally, in a tone that brooked no argument, said, "It's her story to tell."

If Rain had been here, she'd be alerting Tripp to his increased heart rate. But Tripp didn't need his dog to tell him he was upset.

He was all for Cora's privacy. Certainly, he had his own stories he wasn't keen on others hearing until they got to know him better. But he couldn't shake the feeling that if they'd been up front from the start about her story, she wouldn't be sitting in a hospital bed.

But, no. That wasn't right.

He sighed, sat down in the middle of a row of chairs, and put his head in his hands.

He'd failed her. He'd failed them.

He said he'd keep her safe, and the mission was unsuccessful. He was the reason she was sitting in a hospital bed right now, which is why he was going to stay in town and make it up to her over the next month.

When he looked up to the brothers, he said, "This is all my fault. I'm sorry."

Chase and Hunter moved to either side of him. They sat in silence for several minutes, which must have meant they weren't going to tear him apart, that maybe they'd forgiven him.

Hunter let out a long sigh. "It's not your fault. We should have told you, but we couldn't. It's hers to tell."

Tripp understood. Kind of.

The three sat with their own thoughts until Chase finally said, "Hey. I saw Haley Seddington on her way out of the room. Was she just checking on Cora, or is something going on at Four Cross?"

"You guys know each other?"

"I met her at church a while back. She helps out at the ranch sometimes."

Though not his favorite topic, an attempt to change the subject might be appreciated by all. "She helps out at the ranch? She's my half sister."

His friend looked surprised, then nodded. "I remember a photo you showed me on deployment of the two of you. She was pretty young at the time."

"Fourteen years between us. We shared the same mom." *Shared.* It'd been five years since their mom had died and it still felt odd to talk about her in the past tense.

Chase shifted in his seat. "You guys close?"

"Not exactly," he hedged, not mentioning that the last time he saw her was three years ago, when she yelled at him to mind his own business and stay out of her life. "I'm hoping to get some time with her while I'm here."

"It's good that you showed up. She'll need extra support in the months to come."

Tripp opened his mouth to ask him what that meant exactly when Dr. Evans came out of the double doors. "Cora Cross's family?"

Chase and Hunter pushed out of their seats and stepped forward.

She smiled, the wrinkles around her eyes crinkling. "Cora said her protective twin brothers would probably be in the waiting room. I'm Dr. Samantha Evans."

They shook hands while Tripp stood in the background. He didn't even pretend like he wasn't listening.

The doctor clasped her hands together. "I generally prefer to see Cora in the hospital when she's brought someone in to have a baby, not when she's injured."

"She doing okay?" Chase asked.

Smiling, Dr. Evans said, "She's very happy her discharge papers are almost completed and wanted you all to know she'll be ready to leave soon."

"How bad is the ankle?" Chase asked.

Tripp declined to point out if they hadn't been berating him, they'd already know the answer to this question.

"She tore some lateral ligaments. But no worries. If she follows protocol, she won't need surgery."

"Protocol?" Hunter grunted.

"She'll need to stay in a medical boot for the next four weeks."

"How's she going to handle that?" Chase asked.

"Not well," said Hunter muttered.

The men thanked the doctor, and she disappeared through the waiting-room door.

"I'm going to say goodbye to Cora." Chase flicked two fingers to Tripp, separated from Hunter, and headed in her direction.

Tripp ground his molars and returned to his chair. His hands itched to pet his dog, something his body now subconsciously looked for when he felt stressed. But he wasn't worried about his heart condition. He was worried about Cora.

No matter what the diagnosis, that spitfire wasn't going

to want any doctor to tell her to slow down. He had a feeling her ankle was going to require just that.

Because of him.

While Hunter poured himself a cup of free hospital coffee, Tripp texted his client at Four Cross Ranch to let them know he was running late. He also texted Haley, asking her if she wanted to have dinner with him tomorrow.

There was no response.

He got up, walked to the window, and stared at the mountains in the distance. What was Haley doing up here in Wyoming, anyway? The last time they saw each other, he had just separated from the military and visited her at her dad's house in Colorado Springs.

He didn't think she knew anyone in Wyoming.

Actually, he didn't know much about his half sister at all, just that she'd idolized him when she was little and despised him when she got older.

That had felt like a punch in the gut. A bruise that didn't seem to heal over the last three years.

"I need to go check on something at the ranch," Hunter said, "but Cora might get discharged before I can get back. Are you staying a while?"

"I've got her. I'll take her home."

"You don't have to be her chauffeur."

"Actually, that's exactly what I'm going to be."

Hunter raised his eyebrows in question.

"It's my fault she's in this predicament. I told her I'd stay and help her for the next four weeks."

"That's generous of you."

"Probably make the roads safer while she's not behind the wheel."

A smile tugged at Hunter's mouth. "Enjoyed her driving, did you?"

"She should come with a surgeon-general warning."

"We told you she had a heavy foot."

A heavy foot. An inclination toward taking a curve like a NASCAR driver. A complete disregard for general road safety. And a glint in her eye that made Tripp want to stick around to see what came next.

Hunter glanced back at the doors as if Cora was going to come barreling out any second. He looked back to Tripp. "Since you're staying in town a while, maybe we could pick your brain a little."

"Not sure what's left of it," Tripp said, "but whatever's still in there, you're welcome to. What's on your mind?"

"We'd eventually like the nonprofit to have its own division that trains and provides therapy dogs for veteran families. I've started the process, but it's a lot to handle while working full-time on the ranch. I'd appreciate your thoughts."

"Be more than happy to give you my two cents."

"Thanks. I'll touch base." He dipped his chin to Tripp. "See you around."

But before Hunter left the room, something sparked in Tripp's memory from their earlier conversation. "Hey, I wanted to ask you something. Chase mentioned something about knowing Haley from church?"

The last Tripp knew, Haley's dad wouldn't take her to church. He felt better knowing she had gotten plugged into a community again.

"I think that's how Chase crossed her path," Hunter said, pulling keys out of his pocket, "but I first met her at the diner. She's in Cora's Saturday morning group." He turned on his heel and murmured, "See ya later."

Tripp's world stopped spinning.

He no longer heard the low voices of the nearby nurses.

He no longer smelled the stale coffee from the pot in the corner of the room. And he could no longer feel anything.

Instead, Chase's words from earlier came blaring back to him.

It's good that you showed up. She'll need extra support in the months to come.

The dots connected slowly, as if his brain was moving through molasses.

Hunter met Haley in Cora's Saturday morning group. Cora's Saturday morning group consisted of pregnant women from surrounding counties. Chase said Haley would need extra support in the months to come.

Reality hit him square in the chest. Tripp went from feeling nothing to feeling everything.

His nineteen year-old half sister was pregnant.

And Cora had known that when the three of them had talked in her room.

Cora wasn't just going to leave the hospital with a badly sprained ankle. She was going to leave the hospital with a piece of his mind.

Chapter Three

Cora looked at her brother, waiting for his answer. "Chase? Is everything okay with Lexi?" she asked again.

Sitting on the edge of her hospital bed, he held a worried expression, one she'd seen many times on first-time fathers-to-be. "Everything's fine, but I was wondering if you could talk to her?" he asked.

The hairs on Cora's neck raised. She loved her sister-in-law. She also knew that giving birth a little later in life—at age 37—could be hard on the momma and baby.

And just like it always did when a pregnant woman was in need, the world faded away.

Her gifts in midwifery hit her like a storm with strong winds she couldn't ignore. Cora didn't know how others experienced their gifts, but hers gave her no choice. Something inside her heard the call and forced her to focus all of her energy on helping. Which was why she'd even considered visiting the Klines in spite of the heart-stopping fear that their dogs brought. She simply couldn't say no to a baby coming into the world.

She put her hand over his. "What's going on? How can I help?"

Her brother's face softened with relief. "You know Lexi. She's totally capable."

"Yes." Her reply was immediate. Confident. That's what Chase needed to hear. But it was also true of his very talented accountant wife. She was extremely capable.

"But I think that's just it." He rubbed the back of his neck, the stress returning behind his eyes. "She loves her numbers and has a lot of control over pieces of her job and her life. But I think going into a birth where she doesn't have total control is freaking her out."

Or maybe him. But Cora didn't mention it. He didn't need to be reminded of all he'd lost before Lexi came into his life.

She cleared her throat. "I'll set up a time to talk to her."

"If she gets put on bed rest, will you come to the ranch?"

The question seemed innocent enough, but was loaded with history, pain, and memories she wanted to forget. "Is bed rest something the doctor mentioned?"

"Yes."

Her brothers knew the ranch caused flashbacks associated with the scars on her face. She only set foot on the property when absolutely necessary, like now as her gifts called her into the storm once more. "Then, yes," she said quietly. "I'll go if she needs me. You know I will."

Something meaningful passed between them. Something thick, loving, and full of things only siblings would understand after the loss of both parents way too soon.

"Thank you, Coralee," he said gruffly, using her full given name. The one that only her father used with her. The one that now only got pulled out on sentimental occasions by her brothers.

There was a knock at the door and when she said to come in, a very broody Tripp Blackburn entered the room. What was he still doing here? And was he this attractive earlier in the day, or had the stress of being in the MRI death tube done weird things to her?

She couldn't answer those questions, but what she could see was that he was seething over something. His jaw muscles seemed so tense that she was concerned about his molars, and he glared at her while her brother greeted him.

What did Tripp have to be so upset about?

Dealing with her overprotective brothers was bad enough. But Tripp was a wild card. And not the good kind.

"Hey, man," Chase said. "Didn't realize you were still here."

"I'm her ride home." He held her gaze one beat longer than she was comfortable with, but somehow, she couldn't bring herself to look away.

He was her ride home? She guessed that made sense, but she wasn't interested in getting back in the car with him if he was going to be in a mood.

Chase shook his head at Tripp. "I still can't believe after consulting with you over email for over a year and a half, I finally got you to come out here with a dog for one of our veteran families. I'm so glad you're here, man."

Tripp finally broke his stare from Cora and turned to her brother. "Hunter mentioned he wanted to pick my brain about setting up a therapy-dog division at the nonprofit."

"Yeah. That's been his project for quite some time."

"I think it's a great idea and I'd be happy to help you guys sort through all the details." He glanced to her and then back to Chase. "I'll be around for the next four weeks, so we'll have plenty of time to brainstorm."

"It's four weeks now?"

Cora held her breath while she waited for her brother's reaction to the explanation.

"Yeah," Tripp said, "I'm making amends to Cora by being at her beck and call when she needs a ride."

Chase nodded, looking at her with a face that showed approval. She guessed that was better than the fistfight she thought she was going to witness earlier. "Where will you be staying?" he asked.

"I just got off the phone. Your wife made me a deal I couldn't refuse. She said I could stay at the ranch for free."

"She tends to do that," Chase said with a proud smile. "It'll be good to have you close. Lexi's due soon, so I might be busy after that, but I'd love to sit in on those meetings with Hunter until then if I can."

"Two weeks, right?" Tripp whistled. "Getting close."

Chase rubbed his hands together and grinned. "If you ask Lexi, she'll say it's two years."

The men chuckled. But Cora couldn't help herself and, with some attitude, added, "Careful. You guys have no idea what it feels like to be eight and a half months pregnant."

"Why are you so cranky, Cora? You eat your broccoli today?" Chase asked, then explained to Tripp, "She eats half a pound a day."

"I'm cranky because I tore some ligaments in my ankle."

Confusion covered Tripp's face, and it looked like he was trying to calculate a tough math problem. "You eat half a pound of broccoli every day?"

"It's roasted, so it's not that hard to do. I triple-dog-dare you to try it."

"You can't throw down a triple dog dare with me."

"Especially him," Chase confusingly added.

"What if I don't like broccoli?"

Chase looked back and forth from Cora to Tripp, amusement in his eyes and maybe a little bit of mischief.

Deadpan, she said, "Then you'll never know true joy."

Tripp rubbed his hand over his chin. "What about apples? I think I could eat a pound of apples."

"Broccoli and apples are no comparison."

"I know," he said, "one tastes like you're eating a tree root, and the other is actually tasty."

"One gives you more energy than a cup of coffee," she said in her most authoritative tone, "and the other has been used to deceive Eve, Snow White, and the general population with its antics about keeping the doctor away."

At that, a spark hit Tripp's eyes. "I don't think you should be giving nutrition lectures considering your sugar intake on the way to your appointments."

Heat hit her face, and she couldn't hold back a grin. "I would have shared if you'd asked."

"I don't even think you knew I was in the car with you," he teased.

Chase raised his eyebrows to Cora in a big-brother, what-is-going-on-between-the-two-of-you way.

She rolled her eyes and glared at Chase as if to say "Nothing."

What was wrong with her brother? She'd just met the man. Plus, absolutely not. Tripp lived in another state and would be going home in a month. Hopefully, her ankle would heal at light speed and he could go home even earlier. Though for some reason, that idea didn't sit as well as she might have thought.

Chase returned to their conversation. "She's not going to let up, man. I know this from years of experience. Either join the Vegetable Brigade, or let it go."

She snapped her head to her brother. "It's the Broccoli Brigade."

"You get this love of broccoli from Mom, but this half-a-pound-a-day thing happened on Hunter's watch when he took care of you."

"I was a teenager," she said with irony. "It was my rebellious phase."

Chase chuckled, stood, and kissed the top of her head. "I love you. Don't give this guy too much trouble."

"I love you, too," she said as she watched her brother leave the room.

Once she and Tripp were alone, he ran a hand through his hair, causing the already disheveled look to look better than it did before. He paced the room, his expression morphing from very annoyed to conflicted to a softer anger. Then he turned to her and said in a way that sounded like he forced the words out of his mouth, "How are you?"

"Fine." She closed her eyes and on an inhale, she took in the filtered air and the smell of hospital antiseptic.

When she opened her eyes, she found him glaring at her. She crossed her arms and cocked her head. What was going on with him? "Maybe I should ask you the same. How are you?"

"Are you in pain?" he said to her ankle.

Though her medical expertise mainly dealt with pregnant women, it didn't take formal training to know that all of the blues and purples developing over her swollen skin were not a good sign.

"Not as much." She hedged. She wouldn't let his question deter her. Even if it was kind. "I'm going to ask again. How are you?"

When he finally locked eyes with her, he asked, "Why didn't you tell me?"

She balked. What a bizarre question from someone she hardly knew. Then the events of the morning flashed through her head. Was he asking about why she didn't tell him she was injured? Or did he know why she panicked this morning at the Klines? But he seemed angry. Why would he be angry at her? Slowly, she replied, "Why didn't I tell you what?"

"Earlier," he growled. "Why didn't you tell me?"

Okay. He *was* referring to this morning. He wanted to know why she didn't tell him about her aversion to dogs, which was humiliating.

She pushed a button on the inside of her bedrail and raised the head of the bed so she was closer to eye level with him. The sound of the electric hospital bed tried and failed to cut the tension between the two of them. Who was she kidding? She'd have to be standing on a small ladder to look him in the eye, but right now she needed any advantage she could get because his cold stare raked over her.

Her nerves hummed, but she tried to control her voice. "I was scared."

"Scared? What in the world were you scared about?"

"What in the world was I..." She gnawed on her bottom lip, trying to work out what was happening. Her ankle throbbed to the beat of her rising frustration. "You talked to Hunter."

"Yeah," he scoffed. "I just talked to Hunter in the waiting room. But he didn't tell me anything."

Hunter wasn't one to talk much about anything, and she knew from years of experience that he wouldn't tell her story. Which meant she was on her own here.

"You want me to spell it out for you?" She looked out the window, searching for words she certainly couldn't find in her hospital room. When she figured out there was no way around telling him, she whipped her head back to him and blurted, "I'm terrified of dogs! Is that it? Is that what you need to hear? You saw it for yourself. Do you actually need to hear the words from me?"

Tears welled up her eyes, and, if it was possible, she felt more humiliated.

He blinked. Almost as if he was confused. Then his face softened, his blue eyes blazed into hers, and he shook his head slightly. "That's not what I meant," he said almost so softly she didn't hear.

Frustrated, embarrassed, and a little bit angry, she yanked on her blanket to straighten it out, but it caught on her injured foot. Pain shot up her leg. She hissed, closed her eyes, and clutched her calf. When life felt bearable again, she let go of her leg and flopped back into the bed. She tunneled her hands through her hair and held it back from her face. After releasing one final breath, she looked to Tripp.

Only he wasn't looking at her. Or he was, but his focus was on her left temple. A painful combination of concern and compassion filled his eyes as he gently stepped forward and lifted his hand. Slowly.

She knew.

She knew what he saw, and she released her hair so it fell like a curtain over her scars, over her story. She reached for and clutched his wrist before he could touch the three scars at her temple.

They stared at each other for moments until Cora finally released her hold. "Sorry," she murmured.

Tripp pulled a chair up to her bed and sat. He shook his head and looked at her, his face full of regret. "Cora, I owe you an apology."

"Why?"

"I didn't keep you safe this morning. And now, you're here. Injured." His eyes seared into hers. "Please forgive me."

Who was Tripp Blackburn? She had never experienced

a man so wired for battle and full of empathy at the same time. And she was a little bit disappointed she'd been so angry earlier when he asked if she was pregnant. Maybe Tripp was just bad at first impressions. What would life be like with someone like Tripp as her friend?

"Thank you." She looked to her hands in her lap, then back to him. "But I don't think this morning was your fault."

He didn't seem relieved. In fact, he only seemed concerned. His gaze was alert, but it held a sheen of guilt.

Maybe he was someone safe. Maybe she could share. Maybe she *should* share because this man before her, this good man, did not deserve to blame himself for something that wasn't his fault.

She took a breath and whispered her confession. "I never see it coming."

He leaned in. "You never see what coming?"

"I never see anything coming." She cleared her throat to explain but thought better of it and shook her head. He didn't need to hear her life story. "For sure, I never saw the dogs coming. I forgot about Jekyll and Hyde until they were upon me. And then I froze."

She wanted to yell at her seventeen-year-old, terrified, teenager self for her juvenile reaction to canines.

"You said you never see them coming," he said in a gentle voice. "This has happened before." It was a statement. Not a question.

She nodded but wouldn't look him in the eye.

"I should have known." He sat back in his chair, shaking his head. "I'm sorry. I should have figured it out, and I should have adjusted my approach."

"With the dogs?"

"With you."

Bristles of frustration skittered down her spine. "What's that supposed to mean?"

Without missing a beat, he asked, "Do you know what I do for a living?"

"No."

"I'm a highly specialized dog trainer. I work with a wide variety of breeds to be service dogs and therapeutic pets, catering to the needs of each household." She started to say something, but he cut her off when he softened his voice and said, "And I was in a K-9 unit in the army. I have field experience working with soldiers with PTSD. Now, I train dogs to work with veterans adjusting to home life. And I know the signs."

Heat hit her face. "I don't have PTSD."

"No. But you've had a serious trauma involving a dog."

She swallowed and whispered the correction. "A wolf."

Darkness covered his features. "A wolf," he groaned. Waited a beat. Took a breath. Then softened his face again. "So it doesn't surprise me that you froze this morning. I saw the signs when we arrived on the property, but I didn't put them together quickly enough so I could help you. I'm sorry."

"I still don't think it's your fault," she said, her voice a little shaky.

"We'll have to agree to disagree on that. I know the signs of fight, flight, or freeze."

She blanched at the words. "My counselor talked to me about those three reactions once. Why do I have to freeze? It feels like the most embarrassing of the three options. Why can't I fight to the death, or run away with the speed of a gazelle? Those are more impressive."

A smile hitched on the edge of his mouth. "I don't think

you need to look impressive when you're working through trauma."

"At least it would look like I was trying."

He paused and studied her. A question formed behind his eyes before he asked, "Have you kept your distance from dogs ever since?"

She knew what was coming. "I know it doesn't make sense. A wolf isn't a dog."

"Short. Four legs. Claws. Teeth. Can't speak the human language." He gentled his voice. "I get it."

She stared at him, and he let her hold his gaze. Relief hit her when she realized that he really understood her. "Thank you for saying that. And to answer your question, yes. I've tried to keep my distance from dogs. Though it's kind of hard to grow up on a ranch with herd dogs, Hunter did his best to keep them clear of me. When I graduated from high school, I wanted my own place, but I also wanted to get away from the memories. And when I moved off the ranch, I vowed not to return. So, yes, I absolutely avoid dogs at all cost. They're too unpredictable."

"Ever thought about getting one as a puppy and training them to your needs?"

Her understanding of his job locked into place, and she was not on board. He was going to try to convert her to being a dog lover.

Absolutely not.

She held up her hand. "Please do not try to change me. I get that you train dogs for a living, but I'm not interested."

His face remained blank, but so much energy emanated off him, it was like she knew what he was thinking.

"I tried," she said. "I did all kinds of research on breeds to find the perfect one for me. I started with boxers because they're protective. But they scared me. Then I looked at schnauzers and Maltipoos. I just couldn't find what I was looking for."

"Which was…"

With a straight face, she said, "A smart dog who doesn't bark, shed, scratch, bite things, get excited, jump on me, and who knows exactly what I need in the moment."

His smiled. "There's totally a breed for you like that."

"There is?"

"Sounds like you need a fluffy stuffed-animal dog."

Something sparked in his eyes, then they both laughed. It felt good. Not just to lighten the mood. But to laugh. With Tripp.

When their laughter turned to soft chuckles, then to silence, they sat in their thoughts. Something suddenly occurred to her.

"Can I ask you a question?"

"Sure." He sat back in the chair, stretched out his long legs, and crossed them at the ankle.

"You seemed angry when you came into the room. Was something wrong?"

All signs of relaxation left his body. He crossed his arms and stared at her.

"I'm sorry. You don't have to answer that."

Finally, he sighed. He uncrossed his arms, sat up, and clutched the chair as if bracing for something. "Haley's pregnant, isn't she?"

He seemed so earnest. So concerned.

She wanted to tell him. But she was caught behind her professional responsibilities and the privacy that Haley was due.

She said nothing.

"I know. If you're her midwife, and I know she attends your Saturday brunch, you can't tell me anything." He ran his hands through his hair several times, as if he could rid himself of the stress. "I came in here ready to go toe-to-toe with you because you hadn't said anything earlier."

"If I did know, it's not like we had a lot of time to discuss the matter. As I recall, my brothers stormed in the room right after Haley left."

He nodded, staring at the floor. "You're right about that."

"When's the last time you even talked to Haley?" The question was benign. It admitted no knowledge on her part. But she wanted to help, so she'd go at it a different way other than breaking Haley's confidentiality.

"Do you mean real conversations? Or short texts that lead to nowhere?" When she didn't respond, his shoulders slumped, and he finally said, "A while."

"And now you have a business that allows you to be away from home and you're in town for four weeks."

"Yes."

She leaned in, caught his eye. "Then maybe it's time to have a real conversation."

Chapter Four

The scars changed everything.

The marks on Cora's face had torn right through Tripp's anger and slashed his heart.

Three days ago in the hospital, he'd been so ready to confront Cora about her knowledge that his half sister was pregnant, and then the sight of those three jagged lines grounded him to the present.

Nearly undid him.

A wolf.

Of course, she was terrified of dogs.

Now, he was going to be her personal chauffeur for the next three and a half weeks. And along with him came a black Labrador retriever.

Not that she knew that. Yet.

Staring out the front window of his beat-up Tahoe at the Elk Run Diner, he blew out a long breath. One thing at a time.

Before telling Cora about his dog she was bound to be terrified of, he was going to have breakfast with his half sister, who wasn't pleased when he asked her to join him. "Wasn't pleased" was putting it lightly. She didn't mask her irritation when he'd called and was quite blunt when she told him she didn't have much time for him.

But she agreed to meet him for breakfast at the diner, so that had to mean something.

Rain sat in the front seat next to him and set her head on Tripp's lap. His dog sensed his stress, sometimes before he did. This time she was right on target. Tripp stroked long lines over her head and down the back of her silky black coat. He didn't need his monitoring watch to tell him his heart rate was slowing down. Peace he couldn't explain came with Rain.

He wanted everyone else to experience that kind of peace.

He especially wanted Cora to.

"One thing at a time, girl," he murmured to Rain. "One thing at a time."

And right now, the one thing he needed to focus on just walked into the diner to have lunch with him.

Haley was wearing jeans and a long Columbia parka, her gait seeming a little slower than what he remembered.

Tripp and Rain hopped out of the SUV. He helped her into a red service-dog vest and attached a leash to her collar. Some dogs didn't care for the vest, but for Rain, it was a signal she was on the job. She sat tall. Each time she wore the vest, it seemed she was ready not just to help him, but to represent all service dogs to each community they visited. As if she was an ambassador.

Tripp provided positive reinforcement and slipped her a small treat from his pocket. As they walked toward the restaurant, he decreased the slack on her leash. "Heel," he murmured as they made their way through the front door.

At the hostess station, his waitress from the other day slid plastic menus into an open-ended wooden box on the wall. Today, her hair was styled into what appeared to be a bee's hive on top of her head. When she looked up, she smiled at him and said, "Hi, precious."

"Hi, Stacy. How are you today?"

"Never better. You back to tackle the Partridge in a Pear Tree?"

His stomach rumbled, but he didn't know if it was nerves or hunger. Still. Food was food. He slapped a hand on his middle. "I might take another run at it if I don't end up eating alone."

"And I see you brought a friend." She looked at Rain and winked at Tripp. "I'm not sure if the rules allow for a puppy dog to help you eat the platter."

The warrior blood in his dog's veins might be insulted at being called a puppy dog. "This is Rain," Tripp said.

Instead of thumping her tail, Rain sat stock-still, eyes ahead. She knew she was on the clock.

"She's a working service dog," he said. "Would you feel comfortable if I brought her into the diner?"

Most didn't pry into the reason he had a service dog. Some assumed he had one for professional reasons. Tripp never cared what others thought—he just wanted them to be comfortable if he had Rain with him. Not everyone reacted well to dogs.

"Good gravy, of course. That would be just fine." She offered him a smile. "What can I do for you today?"

Tripp scanned the dining room and spotted Haley. The blond hair she got from her father flowed in long layers past her shoulders and made a curtain around her bowed head. She fidgeted in the booth.

"I'm meeting my sister." He pointed in her direction. "I'll head on over."

Stacy exclaimed, "Sweet chips and salsa! Is Haley your family? I didn't know that. She is a gem, that girl."

All he knew to do was offer her an awkward smile. He had no idea if Haley truly thought of herself as his family. Something didn't sit right in his stomach when he thought about how she was *his* only family. Maybe he needed her in his life more than the other way around.

When he arrived at the table, Haley looked up from a menu. Her eyes darted from him to his dog and back again. "Hi," she said, her voice sounding like a bundle of tightly woven nerves.

He slid into the seat opposite his sister, gave Rain her command to sit and relax on the floor outside the booth, and then slipped the dog a treat. "This is Rain." This time his girl thumped her tail once.

Haley's mouth gaped. "She's a... She's a service dog..."

"Yes."

Alarm hit his sister's face. "Are you...um, is she yours?"

"She is."

Concern crossed her face. "Are you okay?"

"I am." He hadn't thought through this part. She didn't know about his health issues. Of course, Haley would have questions. "I have a heart condition. She helps me monitor my heart rate."

Haley looked at him with confusion, then picked up a straw, ripped the wrapper off, and picked it apart one small piece at a time. Her discomfort felt like an extra person at the table who refused to leave. She didn't even want to share the Partridge in a Pear Tree breakfast with him, so they both got pancakes.

To be honest, his own discomfort made them a party of four. He wasn't exactly sure how to bring up her pregnancy.

Once Stacy brought them their meals, he hoped he and Haley could ease into deeper conversation. But she shoveled food in her mouth so fast, he was momentarily mesmerized until he figured that her appetite had probably increased because of her pregnancy. Then the chasm between him and his half sister opened up and almost swallowed him whole.

The fourteen years between them never stretched so far as it did now. He no longer knew anything about his kid sister. Maybe this is how she ate her meals now?

He sighed. Might as well dive in. "Do you normally eat this fast?" he asked.

She paused, the last piece of pancake midway to her mouth, and her eyes resembled a deer caught in headlights.

"I only ask," he said, "because the last time we ate breakfast together, you cut up your pancakes into tiny pieces and only finished a third of it."

"The last time you had breakfast with me was after Mom's funeral," she blurted. Her face looked almost as surprised at the words as he felt. But then, hurt slashed through her eyes, crossed the table between them, and hit him square in the chest.

Rain placed her head on Tripp's thigh and her tail thumped twice.

Haley set down her fork and wiped her fingers with her napkin, one at a time. "The last time you had a meal with me was *five* years ago in Colorado Springs after Mom's funeral," she said, her voice taking on strength, "and I asked if I could live with you, and you said no."

"You were fourteen years old. I was in the military," he said, repeating the same excuses he used five years ago. This time, they fell flat even to his ears.

She further wiped the edges of her mouth and said with a helping of anger, "And the last time you had a meal with me, I also tried to tell you that my dad had started drinking."

He stilled. Something terrible churned in his gut. "Haley," he whispered.

"*Three* years ago when you separated from the military and drove through town on your way to move to Denver, I didn't even get an offer of a meal. We got coffee instead," she said, telling him something he already knew. "And you drank it so fast, you didn't give me the chance to tell you that my dad's drinking was worse. Along with all the other things that come with being an alcoholic."

All the other things. Tripp thought he was going to get sick. Three years ago, she would have been sixteen. Tripp had just separated from the military, had no direction for his life, and could barely look into the eyes of a sixteen-year-old girl whom he was afraid would ask to live with him again. How could he take care of her when he barely knew what he was going to do with his postmilitary life?

"I— Haley, I'm sorry."

Her eyes reddened, and tears formed at the edges. "Why did you come here, Tripp? After all this time, three years of sporadic phone calls and texts, why would you track me down?"

Every word she uttered felt like a jab that reminded him of how he'd failed her. Abandoning his half sister was a heavy coat to wear. Even if it was for a good reason.

His throat clogged with emotion. He tried to clear it away, but to no avail. "I wanted to check on you."

The answer must have disappointed her. He had no idea why. But the tears dried up, and her face shuttered like she was closing herself down to him. She pulled a crinkly twenty-dollar bill out of her pocket and threw it on the table. "Well, now you've seen me. Maybe we'll see each other in another five years."

"When your child is four?" he asked before he could think better of it.

She looked stricken, and he immediately regretted his insensitive question.

"Haley," he said, running a hand through his hair, "I'm sorry. I didn't mean to—"

"How did you find out?"

"Someone mentioned seeing you eat here with Cora's Saturday group."

Just then, his phone pinged with a text message alert, but he ignored it.

Nodding, she looked out the window. "I guess I wasn't going to be able to hide it from you for forever," she said.

He picked up her hand and placed her twenty-dollar bill in her palm, closed her fingers, and pushed her fist back toward her. No way was he letting her pay. He didn't know anything about her plans for the future, but he could certainly buy her breakfast. "What can I do to help?" he asked.

Her gaze went from the money in her hand, to him, and back to the window. "I'm making a life here now, Tripp. It's okay. You don't have to feel like you should help."

This time, his phone rang, but again he ignored it. "You're my only family," he said, thinking of her. And then thinking about the baby she was carrying.

She scoffed as she looked at him, a sharpness to her eyes that he didn't care for. "But that's not why you came here, am I right? You came here for work."

His phone rang again. He shoved his hand in his pocket and fumbled to hit the button he knew would make the sound stop.

She slid out of the booth and stood, but he couldn't let her leave. He put his hand on her arm. "It may not be why

I came here. And I'm sorry about that. I truly am. But it's most definitely a part of why I'm staying."

"At the hospital you said four weeks?" Her question was part anger, part confusion and, if he wasn't mistaken, part hope.

"Yes. Four weeks."

Some sort of understanding settled over Haley, and he could feel the moment she put up an emotional wall again. She squared her shoulders and pinched her lips together. "Four weeks." She nodded. "Sure." Another nod. "I hope you have a good four weeks, Tripp. See you around."

As she stormed to the exit, his phone pinged once more. He wanted to take that thing and throw it into the wall.

What just happened? It felt like he'd done something really wrong. What it was, he had no idea. He swept a hand through his hair and looked around the diner.

For someone who had a four-week plan, he sure felt lost.

When his phone rang again, Rain bumped his hand. Even she was annoyed with the sound.

He yanked his cell out of his pocket and caught Cora's name on the screen for incoming calls, then answered gruffly, "Hello?"

"Babies don't wait, Tripp."

He pulled at the back of his neck with his opposite hand. "I'm sorry?"

"Yes, you're going to be sorry if you promised to be my personal driver and Misty Parsons goes into labor and delivers on her front-porch swing while waiting for me to arrive."

He left money to cover their meals and quickly ran out the diner's front door. "I'm sorry, Cora. I'll be at your place in less than five minutes."

"Don't apologize to me. Apologize to the new deputy

chief. It's his wife, and I happen to know he has an aversion to all things medical."

Great. Just great. So far, the first impression he was making on this town was stellar. Over the last few days, he was responsible for a woman's ankle injury, upsetting a single pregnant woman in need, and he might have gotten himself on the bad side of the town's deputy chief of police.

Hustling, he led Rain through the parking lot to his Tahoe, then opened the back and gave his dog the command to get in her crate.

Her eyes dropped and she looked entirely put out with him about having to go into her crate.

Even Rain was mad at him. He just couldn't win with women this morning.

"I can't help it, girl," he murmured while repeating the command to jump into the back of his car. "We're about to pick up a woman who not only thinks I'm an idiot, but she's scared to death of dogs and doesn't know you exist."

The storm was calling her again. A pregnant woman in need. Only she knew this particular pregnancy weather forecast wouldn't hold. Misty Parsons wasn't really in labor. Her Braxton-Hicks contractions had started at twenty weeks, and had continued to now, her thirty-sixth week.

She kept asking how she would know when her contractions were real, and the best answer anyone could give her was that when they were the real deal, she would know.

For Cora, it was the worst part about being a midwife. She had no personal experience to draw from. Her bold intuition mixed with her constant efforts at education kept her at the top of her game.

But sometimes she wished she could give advice based on a pregnancy of her own.

It was not something she thought she'd ever get to do in her lifetime. Not with the scars drawn across her face. Not with her inability to trust someone.

At this very moment, the someone she didn't trust was Tripp Blackburn. Clearly, he didn't understand her job. She was just going to have to spell it out for him.

From her window, she watched his older model SUV veer around the corner and come to a full stop in front of her tiny rental house. She prepared to make a beeline for his vehicle, ready to throw her backpack in the trunk and head toward Misty's house. But her crutches made putting the backpack on difficult.

Three quick knocks sounded at the door and she opened it and let him in. "I can't get the backpack on."

She leaned her weight into the wall of her entryway, and he moved behind her to help her slip the straps over her shoulders.

"Nice place." He glanced around, then stepped toward the bulletin board on her living-room wall full of baby pictures. "You deliver all of these?"

"Yes."

"Wow," he said, staring at the pictures.

For the first time, she wondered what he thought of her. Why it mattered, she didn't quite know, but she definitely wanted to know what he thought of her oversize, nap-worthy couch, or the coffee table from her parents' house, or her mother's favorite books stacked on the shelves.

"Umm," he said, his mouth twitching with a smile as he gestured to the living-room windowsill she was just using as a lookout. "Your plants seem to be struggling."

"I know. I can't keep a plant alive to save my life." She

sighed. "I know I should have let them go a long time ago, but I'm still mourning this round."

"This round," he said, chuckling. "That's ironic, don't you think?"

"Ironic?"

He opened his mouth to say something, clearly something he thought humorous, but she interrupted him. "We need to go."

Except when she stepped on the porch, she realized her mistake. The trek to the car was going to be precarious with her bulky backpack threatening to topple her to the ground.

With a quick nod to her, Tripp murmured, "I got this," and maneuvered each crutch so he could slip the pack off her, then held out a hand to steady her down the stairs.

Once on level ground, she shifted on her crutches and her entire body floated through the next few steps as if thanking her for letting Tripp carry the backpack. Guess she needed to work on her balance. "Hunter said you're staying at one of the new tiny houses for the nonprofit at the back of the ranch. How's that working out?"

"The houses sure are nice. Chase said they weren't booked up and it was no problem to stay for the month." He matched his pace to her slow, clunky one. "And it's great to be so close to a client. I basically walk out my front door and get to work."

"About that," she said, holding back a cringe of guilt. "I feel really guilty that you're here just to drive me around. I'm sure that can't be easy on your dog-training business."

"It's not as hard as you think. I've delegated several things to my employees, and this is actually my slower season. As long as everything runs like it's supposed to back home, I have plenty I can do remotely here to keep the business going." He smiled. "Plus, you can't feel guilty about my staying if I'm here because I feel guilty about your foot. Maybe we should both let go of our guilt and enjoy the day."

"That sounds like a plan." She smiled back, but then said gently, "You were late this morning to pick me up."

"I know. I'm sorry," he said gruffly. His mood had shifted, and tension rolled off him, but it was more than just stress. It was almost a sadness.

"Tripp, are you—"

"I know," he said, trudging to the car ahead of her. "I need to be readily available to you. I got caught up in something. It won't happen again. I promise."

He placed her bag in the back seat, pausing to do something she couldn't see. When she caught up to him, she put a hand on his arm. "I was going to ask if you were okay."

He turned to her, studied her face. "I'm okay. But I'm a little worried you're not about to be."

She drew back. "What's that supposed to mean?"

"First, I want you to know that I have all your necessities." He smiled, and even though it wasn't quite a full-fledged smile, it seemed to be a sincere peace offering. "I brought adapters to plug your phone into my car so you can listen to your crazy playlists. I have an entire stash of Twizzlers. Though I did wonder if you restrict your teeth-killing to licorice, or if any sugar candy will do, so I brought backups. And while I'm not prepared to speed at an Indy 500 pace, I have a dependable GPS in my car and a full tank of gas."

She cocked her head. "What other kinds of candy?"

His eyes sparked, but his face remained all business. "SweeTarts, Hot Tamales, Junior Mints, and Raisinets."

Making the worst face she could muster, she said, "Raisinets? That's just offensive."

"Offensive? How so?"

"Chocolate is the bacon of sweets," she declared definitively. "But it's not a miracle worker."

"I'm sorry, what does that mean?"

She scoffed, not understanding his confusion. "It's a universal truth that bacon makes everything better."

"Agreed," he said.

"And it's also a universal truth that chocolate makes everything better."

"I'll agree for the sake of this discussion."

"And, despite their nutritional value, brussels sprouts are the exception to the Bacon Rule. Nothing helps brussels sprouts. Not even bacon." The lines on his brow creased with perplexity, but she pushed forward. "And chocolate makes everything better. Except for raisins. Nothing makes raisins better."

"But you like salads," he said in a tone that implied she had lost her mind.

She knew where this conversation was headed. She pointed at him. "If you even think of getting me a salad with any kind of dried fruit on it, we'll have words."

"Note to self," he murmured, his lips twitching, "no raisins for Cora. Or any other kind of dried fruit."

She paused, and let warmth fill her chest. She just thought he'd be her ride. But he'd thought of so many details.

"Thank you for the provisions." A small grin tugged at her mouth, but then she remembered how he'd started this conversation. "But a minute ago you said you were worried I wasn't about to be okay. Why is that?"

The question seemed to suck the playfulness out of

their conversation. Tripp's entire demeanor changed. For a long moment, he looked everywhere but at her. Finally, he shoved his hands in his jeans pockets and said, "I have a service dog who goes everywhere with me. She's in a kennel in the back. I don't think you'll know she's there. But I also know that sometimes trauma doesn't care if you're safe now. It only remembers the past."

Her chest squeezed, and finding oxygen suddenly became more difficult. She pulled in the next breath, but said nothing.

"But if this doesn't sit well with you, I have a contingency plan," he said. "Chase is in town on a grocery run for one of Lexi's cravings. He's about a minute away and is on call to take you if you're not comfortable with the situation."

She knew he meant well, but years of frustration pricked at her skin. Most never understood her discomfort around dogs. Over the years, many well-intentioned pet owners had tried to help her. "Why do dog owners always force their good opinions of their pets on other people? Is that what you're doing here? Trying to change me?"

His face softened, and so did his tone. "No, Cora. I'm not. I didn't have time to drop her off at the ranch before I came to get you. But it's your choice to be around her. It will always be your choice."

It was her choice. The words sank deep. Deep enough that the vise squeezing her chest released some of its grip.

With the wolf, it had never been her choice. It was reactionary and traumatic all in the same terrifying moment. But it had never been her choice.

This moment was her choice.

She looked past the road, not focusing on anything, just

letting the situation sink into her bones. *This moment was her choice.* "Will you need to get her out of the crate?"

"No."

She thought better of her question. "Will she be *okay* in the crate?"

Something changed in his face. Something warm and meaningful that she liked, but couldn't define. "She'll be fine. If it's okay with you, I'll let her out while you're in your appointment."

Was that okay with her? A peace settled in her. "Yes. That's fine. Let's do this."

He nodded. With a few additional awkward movements, they maneuvered her and her giant boot into the front seat, and he stowed her crutches in the back seat.

Logic told her that she was safe. Other than some shuffling and sniffing, not a sound was heard from the crate in the back. But her senses went on automatic alert with a dog so nearby. Her brain tried to convince her there was a scary, giant animal in the back, so she peeked, but couldn't exactly see the dog through the small holes in the crate.

She shook her head and took a deep breath to try to exhale out Over-Imagination and its friend, Anxiety.

"Do you know how long the drive is?"

Cora took the question as a welcome distraction, and to answer, set the Parsons's address into his GPS. Tripp maneuvered the SUV in the direction of their country home.

"Do you want to get your phone plugged into my car so you can start your warm-up routine?" he asked.

"My warm-up routine?" Amused, she threw him a smile.

"One list is called 'Pre' and one is called 'Post.' I figured you need your crazy music to help you warm up before the appointment, and then cool down afterward."

"It's not an athletic event, Tripp."

He flashed her a grin. "It is the way *you* drive."

She giggled, then peered out the window. Small-town life transitioned to the snow-coated country fields of the winter. Patches of thick grass poked through the snow. "Each time I go to an appointment, I'm not sure what I'm going to get. A terrified woman in labor. A stressed-out new father trying to maneuver a situation out of his control. A baby who demands to come into this world earlier than expected. But whatever I find when I arrive, it's almost always high emotions, usually coming at me from several angles."

"There's so much at stake."

"Exactly." She turned to look at him. "So when I walk into that situation, I have to be the epitome of calm. Nothing else can matter. Nothing else can rattle me. I have to get all of my own high emotions out before I step one foot into that home."

"You get it out through the music," he murmured, then asked, "But you don't seem rushed to put on music now. This feels different than the trip to the Klines."

"Last time, I could feel my own anxiety. I knew I needed the music."

"Because of the dogs." He nodded his understanding. "Which means, this visit, for whatever reason, isn't as stressful because you don't feel like you need the music."

Road hammered away under the tires of his big truck. The sound reminded her of her own battle cruiser and lulled her body into a peaceful state.

He glanced to her and gentled his voice. "And what about the music on the way home?"

She swallowed. She might as well talk about it. It's not as if he hadn't seen the tears, even if some of those tears were for a torn ankle tendon. "It's a release. Because I can't take all that stress home with me."

The look on his face was one of surprise.

Leaning down to scratch a place on her knee just above her medical boot, she asked, "Why do you look so shocked?"

"It's genius." He shook his head, as if he was trying to get the idea to settle in his mind. "I deal with a lot of clients who are working through something big. It could be PTSD or a sickness or physical need. I'm going to tuck that method away to mention to people who might benefit from that kind of a release."

A comfortable silence settled over the car. The hyperawareness of his dog didn't leave her, but she also felt safe. Still, one thing gnawed in the back of her mind.

"Can I ask you something?" she finally said.

"Sure."

The itch moved farther down her leg, and she pushed her fingers under the top of the boot to scratch.

"You mentioned that your dog is a service dog." She paused, gauging his reaction. He only stared at the road and nodded, so she proceeded. "Is that for professional use when you train people, or for personal use?"

Another small nod. "Personal use. I got bacterial endocarditis while deployed overseas. It caused damage to a cardiac valve, and someday it'll need to be replaced. Rain helps me keep track of how my heart is doing."

The few details she knew about the disease slid into place. But one thing she couldn't process. How would his girlfriend help him monitor his heart?

"Rain?" she asked.

"She's my Labrador retriever."

Of course! *Rain.*

So. Not his girlfriend. Why did that make Cora feel relieved?

"So how does Rain help you?" she asked.

"She can detect anomalies in heartbeats and blood-pressure changes. She knows when my heart is under stress and can alert me. Also, if something were to happen to me, like I collapse or pass out, she knows how to find help."

Concern skittered through her. "Are you worried about those things happening?"

"Not as much as I'm worried about how you're going to get that itch you keep working on." He leaned over, popped the glove box, and retrieved a tire gauge. He smelled like Stacy's apple pie from the diner, a cozy winter day, and a good but scary movie. When his shoulder brushed hers, she wanted to sink into his flannel shirt and watch that scary movie with him.

What was wrong with her?

She was suddenly more aware of this mountain of a man than the dog in the back. Oddly, she felt more scared of the man than his dog. He might have the ability to upend her world worse than Rain.

Once he had the gauge in hand, he leaned back to his seat and the car swerved.

"And you think I'm a bad driver?" she asked.

"I had control of the vehicle the entire time. When you drive, I'm not entirely sure what you have control over." He handed her the tire gauge.

"What am I supposed to do with this?"

"Pull the tiny gauge part out of the middle, then stick that farther in your boot to get that itch."

She did as she was told and the second the instrument hit the itch, she moaned. "You're brilliant."

He smiled but kept his focus on the road.

GPS led him to the Parsons's place. When he slowed the car to turn into the driveway, she took a long cleansing breath.

Tripp parked and walked around the vehicle to grab her crutches and help her get down from the SUV. She didn't know what was worse. His hands on her hips to hoist her up into the car, or their close proximity after he set her down from the car.

He nodded at the house. "Do you need help with this one?"

With both crutches in one hand, she threw her backpack over her shoulder and around her back, then switched hands and put her arm through the other strap. "Just keep the car warm in case I need a quick getaway."

His entire body seemed to go on alert. "What? Why?"

Her lip ticked up in a half smile. "Because I'm probably about to have to tell a very uncomfortable, very pregnant woman that she's not anywhere near labor, and sometimes that doesn't go well."

Chapter Five

A week later, crankiness flowed through Tripp's veins.

Which was probably better for him than the cholesterol now hurling through his bloodstream from his failed attempt at eating a Partridge in a Pear Tree. Again.

Slumped in his booth, he stared at the platter of uneaten food. It mocked him.

So did his phone.

Seven days since he'd seen his sister. Seven days of unanswered calls. Unanswered voice mails. Unanswered texts.

Today, he tried to entice her to talk to him by telling her he'd ordered a Partridge in a Pear Tree and needed her help.

He was pitiful. And useless when it came to his half sister.

She was going to wait him out, then he would leave town and prove to her that he'd abandoned her. Again.

At least his dog forgave easily.

"I know I said that bacon made everything okay, but it feels like you're overdoing it a little," a familiar voice said from twenty feet away. A voice he'd found interesting over the last week. Challenging. Formidable. But in moments given to mommas, babies, and if he was fortunate, himself, her voice could be soothing.

He looked up to find Cora, her head cocked, a smile starting to form at the edges of her mouth. With her backpack over her shoulders, she leaned into her crutches and rocked from side to side. Today, dark blue scrub pants with white stars were paired with a red puffer jacket on top. The removable boot allowed her to layer underneath her scrubs for the Wyoming winter. And a wool sock poked through the end of her boot. But he always worried the toes on her injured foot would get too cold.

"What are you doing here?" he asked. "I thought I was picking you up at your place to take you to your next appointment?"

"Part of the Velcro on my boot tore off. Hunter was around, had a little extra time on his hands, and took me to get a new one. When we saw your truck in the parking lot, he dropped me off here so you wouldn't have to make a trip to my house."

Why did it bother him that she didn't call him about her boot?

Simple. Because in the last week, he'd enjoyed running her all over three counties. That enjoyment was unexpected. Pleasant. Maybe even meaningful. Cora continued to show him who she was, and he could admit he was more than intrigued. She was an imposing woman, but had a soft side that she showed few people.

In fact, more often than he wanted to admit to himself, he found himself thinking about the spitfire with the injured ankle rather than his business and life back home in Colorado.

She eyed the iPad and keyboard he had set up in front of him. "Working?"

He scrubbed a hand over his face. "Kind of. I was checking my email. My breeder is on track with his next round of puppies, but there might be issues with the foster families."

"Foster families?"

"I usually have three to five families who, at one time or another, take in some of my puppies to house-train and give them a foundation of commands to follow. They let me know how the pups are doing, and what kind of temperaments we're looking at. It makes a difference in how and what I train them to do. After their training is complete, they're fostered again while I work to connect them with their future owners. Sometimes I cater their foster care to the needs of the new owners."

Cora just stared at him, something working behind her beautiful eyes. He waited, at ease under her scrutiny, hoping she would become more and more comfortable with him. With the dogs. Okay, definitely with him.

"And is everything okay with your new litter?" she asked.

"The litter is fine. I'm only getting two of the golden retriever puppies from my breeder's latest. But one of my foster families might have to back out of their commitment to help. That puts a wrench in things because the other families I work with are unavailable."

Her eyebrows drew down, and she looked concerned. "I'm worried that your staying in Wyoming is costing your business more than you're letting on."

"That's kind of you to say, but it's not. I'll get things covered."

"But will you have to go home early?" Her question punched him in the gut. He didn't want to go home. Even after just a week and a half in Elk Run, he was getting attached to this small town. Its people. Maybe even a certain strong-willed brunette.

"I hope not," he said, keeping her eyes held in his.

Waitress-extraordinaire Stacy passed in front of Cora, carrying a tray with two giant plastic cups filled with ice and a dark, carbonated beverage. Her face was full of concern, and she looked from him to Cora. "He tried to eat it by himself. Bless his heart."

Cora's eyes grew big. "Why in the world would you do that? My brothers can't even finish the thing together."

Tripp rubbed his hands on his jeans, then rested them on the tops of his thighs. "Your brothers told me that you were the only one in the family to have earned the infamous Partridge in a Pear Tree dessert."

She straightened her spine to stand tall and proud. All five foot, few inches of her petite self. "It's true. I did."

"But they said that you cheated."

"Cheated?!" Her mouth hung open.

"The rule is no more than four people. You ate the platter with three pregnant women. That's seven total people."

Her shoulders shook with laughter.

He grinned and nodded to the seat across from him in the empty booth. "I think you should join me and prove you can follow the rules and really do it."

"I'm not enabling you," she quipped. "You're going to have to earn that dessert on your own. But I did come in here to grab a salad before we head out."

She took two crutch-aided steps, then stuttered to a stop. Her eyes saw Rain, then she looked to him. "Oh, um… I can eat at the counter."

As she walked away, reality hit him. He'd been so surprised to see Cora, he'd completely forgot about Rain. Until now, he'd done a good job of keeping them separated.

"Cora." He slid out of the booth, gave Rain the signal to stay, then slowly walked to her.

She turned, didn't take her eyes off Rain, and cleared her throat. "Yes?"

"I can tell her not to pay attention to you," he said softly, so the other patrons wouldn't hear. "I promise. She won't even acknowledge you."

Her gaze remained locked on Rain. "She's beautiful," she whispered.

Now, why did that compliment make something in his chest warm? Just like those rare moments with her soothing voice. Things might not be going well with Haley, but he wasn't complaining about being the warrior-princess midwife's taxi driver.

"Thank you," he said. "And she's highly trained. I can tell her not to come near you."

Her brow crinkled, but she still looked at Rain. "That makes me sound like a terrible person, doesn't it?"

"No, it doesn't," he said, scratching his chin, "And it doesn't have to be forever. Each time you see her, I can communicate my expectations to her."

"So you're telling me that if I sit across the booth from you, she won't jump on me, put her claws on me, lick me, or try to eat my food?"

"She won't eat your food because bacon beats a salad any day of the week that ends in *y*." Cora giggled, and he felt grateful she was releasing some of the tension she'd held since she caught sight of his dog. "But she won't approach you unless I tell her it's okay."

Tripp had no intention of forcing his dog on her. But this is what he did for a living. If he could play even a small role in helping her feel more comfortable around animals, he was all in.

Cora finally looked to him, her hazel eyes boring into his. "Okay," she said quietly. Confidently.

This woman was the bravest person Tripp had come across since his days in the military.

She delivered babies for a living. As she'd just done two days ago. After a long labor and no small amount of pressure from the family. She literally helped bring life into the world. Tripp would crater under all that responsibility.

And today, standing in a small Wyoming diner, she seemed to decide that she would take a step toward her biggest fear.

"Stay here for just a second." He squeezed her on the shoulder and walked toward Rain.

After pulling a treat from his pocket, he squatted down and offered it to Rain. She chomped the treat and thumped her tail twice on the linoleum.

Using both hands, he rubbed Rain from her ears down to her neck the way she liked it best, causing her tags to lightly clink. She squinted her eyes while her head lolled back and forth, and she smiled. "Okay, girl. I know you know what you're doing. Let's take good care of Cora, alright?"

Rain licked him on his cheek.

"I know you want to love on her," he murmured, "but I need you to protect her from a distance."

One more treat, and Tripp stood. "Work," he said.

Rain sat at attention, tall and proud, and focused on Tripp.

Tripp walked to Cora, crouched, and ran his hand down in a straight line, palm facing Cora, from her knee to the floor. "Away," he said. Then he repeated the motion and word one more time.

Rain stayed at attention.

"Why did you train her to keep away from others?" Cora asked.

"Because you're not the only one I work with who's scared of dogs. It's important that everyone feels safe around Rain. And around me." He placed his hand on the small of her back. "You ready?"

She nodded, and they walked to the booth together.

Over the course of the last week, everything felt good about supporting Cora. She was funny, even when she didn't know it. And he continued to sit back and just wonder what she would do next. He'd never been around a woman like her before.

Balancing on one foot, she maneuvered her crutches and hung them on the tall coat hook attached to the booth, then whipped off her backpack and threw it to the vinyl cushion. The entire event took less than three seconds, and she looked like Wonder Woman of the Winter West just taking care of business.

She was larger than life. It's like no one told her she was tiny.

Once they were settled, Cora ordered her salad, and Tripp studied her.

"Why are you staring at me?" she asked.

He crossed his arms and leaned into them on the table. "You are a woman of contradictions."

"I am not," she said through soft laughter.

"You are."

Her eyes widened, and her face flushed with pink. Tripp liked that, too.

"You're ridiculous." She unrolled her silverware from the napkin. "I grew up in this town—I've had the same job my entire adult life, lived in the same rental house. There's nothing contradictory about me."

He picked up a rasher of crispy bacon and pointed it at her. "You order salads and lecture your brothers on eating their vegetables, but consume enough Twizzlers en route to appointments to keep you on a sugar high for three days."

Her lips pursed, and it looked like she was holding back a smile.

"You bring life into this world on a regular basis," he continued, "but you can't keep a plant alive to save your life."

Picturing every last attempt at greenery dead on her porch and front hallway, she couldn't come up with a way to refute his observations, so she shoved a bite of salad in her mouth, chewed, and glared at him.

"You could do without adults, but the second you lay eyes on a baby, your entire world changes."

Her face softened, and he held her gaze.

Memories of her cradling the newborn would be burned in his brain for a long time. He'd never seen such a look of awe, wonder, and pure, unfiltered love. It took his breath away. And maybe a piece of his heart.

"And my guess is," he said gently, "that even though dogs terrify you, you'd run through a pack of them to get to someone in distress."

He hadn't planned to push her to tell her story. But something clicked.

"Where were you going that night, Cora?" he asked.

She blinked. "What?"

"The night the wolf attacked you," he said softly. "Where were you going? Was it to help someone?"

What was it with Tripp's questions? He hurled them at her like a barrage of grenades.

"First of all, if I'm a woman of contradictions, it's not my fault. Maybe it was because I was raised by so many different people. My momma and daddy died when I was sixteen. Hunter left the military to come home and raise me, but Chase and his now-deceased wife, Laura, weren't far behind on the train of people who had a parental role in my life."

The only person who'd never acted like her parent at one time or another was her younger brother, Ryder. He reminded her how to be a kid again. Even as he grew into adulthood.

"No one could live my life, experience the influence of so many different people, and escape contradictions," she said.

"I bet that's right. Were you there to help someone that day of the attack?" he asked, gently repeating his question.

After clanking her fork on her plate, she sat back and crossed her arms. "I think you give me too much credit."

"How so?"

Her face turned hot, but she knew it wasn't the same blush from earlier. This heat felt blotchy. Angry. She wiped her mouth with her napkin and shook her head. "Okay. You know what? I'll tell you. But only because you're being nice about your dog. And because I can't stand the thought of you making me out to be a saint."

He dropped his uneaten piece of bacon and speared a look into her. "I'm not trying to make you out to be anything."

On a sigh that felt almost painful, she set her elbows on the table, bowed her head, and placed her forehead in her hands. "I snuck out."

"I'm sorry?"

She lifted her gaze and looked at him. "I was seventeen. My parents had died the year before. Hunter had left the army to come home and take care of Ryder and me. I was supposed to hang out with his boring farmer friends from high school, but instead, I snuck out to see a boy my brother had forbidden me to see."

Tripp's eyes filled with compassion. "Okay," he said softly.

"Okay?" Her tone rose. Did he not understand? "I snuck out. Lied. Was supposed to be with my big brother's protective friends, but instead I went to meet my secret boyfriend and got attacked by a wolf. I'm pretty sure I deserved what I got."

He blinked. Cocked his head. "What happened to the boyfriend?"

Her eyes focused out the window, unseeing the mountains she knew were there. Instead, her head replayed the image of Grant's back when he ran from her. "He got away. Unhurt."

"Seems to me if you believe you got what you deserved, that would mean he would've also gotten what he deserved. But that's not the case."

She looked to Tripp.

"You went out there to help him," he said, and she stayed quiet. "Didn't you?"

She finally nodded. "He lived with his daddy. Who hit him. We—" She inhaled and released a breath. She'd never told anyone this part. "I was taking him money so he could run away. He had a job waiting in Montana. The plan was for him to set up his life and keep in touch. I'd join him after graduation."

"But he abandoned you." Something in Tripp's voice was heavy, gruff.

"It all happened so fast. One second Grant was there. The next, he wasn't. And in his place were the wolves." She could still hear the caustic barks, feel the panic in her veins, and smell her fear.

Tripp said nothing, but took her hand in his solid grip and rubbed his thumb over her knuckles, grounding her to the present. To the diner. To him, his touch, and his presence.

"I didn't see them coming." She offered him a sad smile and shrugged, thinking not just about the wolves, but about her life. Her parents' deaths. Ryder's leaving the ranch to go on the rodeo circuit after high school graduation. And just last week, the Klines's dogs. "I never see it coming. Anything in life, I just never see it coming."

He sat up and leaned toward her. "You never see it coming because that's who you are. You exist in the present moment. Not in the past. Not in the future. I've seen it all week with you and your work. Even your relationships. Everything is in real time."

She felt exposed, but also somehow known. And a little bit confused. "What do you mean?"

"Everyone's wired differently. You orient yourself to the present. You have no tolerance for anything else, and your entire life is set up around that. You even picked a career that depends on you understanding the present moment. Some people can't stand to sit in the present. It's too painful. But you thrive on it. Base your life around it. It's a strength, Cora."

"It's the babies," she whispered. "Everything disappears when the babies come. They're brand-new and pure and beautiful. Nothing else matters when a new life comes into the world. Yes. I trust each moment holds everything it needs and it's going to be okay." But she scoffed. "However, it didn't feel like a strength when the wolves showed up."

His eyes narrowed, and he studied her. "Do you trust God? Is that how you stay in the present?"

That question raised the hair on the back of her neck. She pulled her hand from his. "I think this discussion is over."

He ran a hand down his face and looked put-out with himself. "I'm sorry. I only ask because if you trust that each moment holds everything it needs and is going to be okay, there must be some piece of you that trusts God to help you with whatever that moment brings."

If she trusted God with each moment, she wasn't in touch with that part of her. What she knew and understood was that she had become excellent at what she did for a living. She depended on her abilities. Because who truly understood when God showed up and when He didn't?

But Tripp didn't let up. "And there must be some piece of you that can see that even when you were in the moment on a hillside with Grant, God took care of you because you're still here."

Still here. And scarred.

And superperturbed at one inquisitive, handsome, former military, dog trainer.

Also...intrigued.

She crossed her arms and glared at him.

"Sorry." He looked over her shoulder, then back to her. "I'm trying to work something out on my own side of things. Maybe I overstepped. Between my half sister and you, I'm starting to wonder if I should avoid talking to women altogether. Clearly, I'm doing something wrong."

Everything in Cora's body went on alert as if it sensed an impending storm. "What's wrong with Haley?"

A smile tugged at one side of Tripp's mouth. "See? Present tense. It's like a beacon."

"What's wrong with Haley?" she repeated.

"I can't seem to build a bridge with her to save my

life." He picked up the piece of bacon he had dropped, took a bite.

She chewed on another forkful of salad and studied him. A man who'd lived a life in the military probably didn't have much experience with pregnant women. Or babies. Or a younger half sister. But instinct told her his heart was good, through and through.

While eating in companionable silence, Cora chewed on thoughts about Haley and Tripp. She couldn't betray Haley's medical confidence, but she might be able to help a little. She grabbed a napkin from the dispenser and wiped her fingers one at a time.

"I imagine it must be a lot to take in, finding out your young sibling is pregnant. Unmarried," she said.

Tripp grunted an agreement, grabbed his own napkin, and swiped it over his mouth.

"I'm wondering," she said, feeling like she was tiptoe-ing through a minefield, "if you've thought about things from Haley's perspective."

Sparks flew from his eyes. "How can I do that if she won't even talk to me?"

"So it's her fault?"

"Yes." He huffed, then calmed down. "No… I don't know."

"You don't know?"

Vulnerability filled his eyes, and for one quick moment, the warrior across the table looked defeated. "She wanted to come live with me when I was in the military. Our mom had died, and I didn't know things had gotten so tough for her with her dad, and I told her no. How was I supposed to raise a teenager when I was on deployment?"

A deep understanding about her own life dawned on Cora. "You weren't," she said through a thick throat.

Which is why Hunter had separated from the military to raise her and her brother. Watching Tripp process the impossible choice gave Cora compassion for Hunter. She hadn't understood his sacrifice. Not fully. And sitting here in the Elk Run Diner, that sacrifice weighed heavy.

Tripp stared at her. "But I got home and have spent the last three years focusing on starting and running my business, when I should have reached out to her and made a better effort to be a part of her life. Then maybe this wouldn't have happened."

A small smile hit her lips. One that she couldn't control even if she had wanted to. "Do you mean maybe that blessing of a baby wouldn't be with her?"

A look of bewilderment crossed his face. "Blessing?"

"All babies are blessings," she whispered, tears glistening her eyes. "I see it every day. These tiny creatures who have the capacity to change others. Show them love. Give them perspective. Offer them grace. They're powerful tiny things."

Tripp studied her. It felt like he was looking deep into her soul. And she let him. She couldn't explain much in life. Didn't understand how God worked. But she knew babies. And she wasn't afraid of Tripp seeing that her words were true.

"I think," she said softly, so the words wouldn't trample him, "that maybe this baby will be a blessing for you, too."

With his voice low, he asked, "Let's say I'm willing to entertain that thought. How will I know if she won't even talk to me?"

She swallowed. "You're going to have to stick around, ask her questions, offer her all kinds of grace, and help her, even if she doesn't ask for the help."

His entire demeanor changed. "What kind of help?" he asked with a little more confidence.

Ah. The soldier wanted something tangible to do. Good. "She'll need maternity clothes."

His face blanched. "You want me to go shopping for her?"

Cora giggled. "As much as I'd like to see what you would pick out for a pregnant woman to wear, I was going to suggest buying her gift cards."

Stacy brought the check by, and before Cora could react, Tripp pulled his wallet out of his back pocket and threw a generous amount of cash on the ticket. Chivalrous and generous. Her annoyance for the former soldier was becoming harder to tamp down.

"I can do a gift card," he said.

"That'll be a good start. We can talk about more concrete ways to support her after we see how that goes."

"What if that goes poorly?"

"Then we pull out the big guns."

His eyebrows drew down in question.

She struggled to lug her medical-boot-clad foot and scooted out of the booth. True to Tripp's word, Rain remained still. She appeared uninterested in Cora, but held an underlying alertness of her owner.

"Then we'll figure out her favorite food cravings," Cora explained.

"Okay," he said, getting up from the table and nodding. "Okay. I like that plan."

She liked it, too. They were working together, and not just about seeing her clients. They were working through issues with his sister. And he seemed to be able to be both strong and gracious about Cora's past. Something was growing between the two of them. Something that felt significant. She wondered if he felt it, too.

Would his job send him home before they could figure out what that something significant could turn into?

Chapter Six

Standing outside the doctor's office, Tripp took in the sight. Cora's face and her entire demeanor beamed. In reality, she clunked through the door he held open and onto the sidewalk with the sway to her gait so one-sided that he held out his hands, ready to catch her if she fell.

"So," he said, positioning himself better to grab her if she got off balance, "looks like the doctor's predictions panned out. It's been two weeks, and you were released from the crutches."

"Isn't it great?" She flashed a smile at him, then took another awkward step and swayed to the right.

He grabbed her elbow. "I gotcha."

"I'm okay. You don't have to hold on to me."

"Still," he said, his mouth twitching to hold back a smile, "I'd feel better if I helped."

"Whatever."

When they were a few steps from his SUV, she paused. "I bet I could try driving. I would just have to get used to the heaviness of the boot—"

"Absolutely not." This woman couldn't drive even when she *wasn't* wearing a medical boot. No telling what trouble she could get into with a heavier foot at the helm.

Once they were settled in the SUV, Cora's phone rang. She glanced at the caller ID and answered, "Hi, Chase."

After a pause, her face morphed into concern. "Put Lexi on the phone, Chase."

Slowly, oh, so slowly, she closed her eyes. Tripp went on alert and fired up the engine.

She looked to Tripp and said into the phone, "I'm on my way."

When she disconnected, she stared out the side window.

"Where are we headed, Cora?"

"I can smell the storm," she whispered.

"What does that mean, sweetheart?"

She looked at him, a hint of fear in her eyes. "We need to go to Chase's house. Four Cross Ranch. Now."

The ranch.

She was going to return to the ranch. Not just any part of the ranch, but the back half, which came up against the property line. In the spot where, once upon a time, she'd encountered a wolf, although it now was the site of Chase and Lexi's new house, Hunter's home, and the guest cabins of the family nonprofit Four Cross Hope, where Tripp was currently staying.

He'd never been so grateful he'd remained in town to help her than at this moment. She was strong. She'd handle this. But if he happened to be by her side just in case she needed a little extra support, he was glad for it.

"It's not like I thought this day would never come." She offered a small smile that didn't reach her eyes. "It'll be okay. Lexi needs me right now."

He nodded, then backed the vehicle out of the parking space. But while he drove away, he put his hand over hers to offer her strength.

The second that Tripp aimed his truck in the direction

of the ranch, Cora shut down. No outrageous music blared through his speakers today. In her own world, Cora had pulled her hair back into a ponytail, showing the three scars for the world to see. Something she rarely did. In his recent experience carting her around the county, he'd observed that she only did that during actual deliveries, when nothing mattered to her except her care of the baby and momma.

But every now and then, her hair would be down and pulled back in a way that exposed the scars. She'd quickly shift some hair to cover the evidence of the wolf.

He counted it a privilege if she let him see her scars. It was clear she didn't view it the same way.

But in this moment, she seemed to be locked inside a tension so overwhelming, she either didn't realize or didn't care that he could see the marks on her face. Which had him on alert.

Once again, he was thrown into protection mode for a Cora whose focus had spun tightly into the present moment.

And once again, he didn't mind this role at all. Kind of hoped it might be his role a little more often in the future.

Except that wouldn't work. Long-distance relationships never worked. Plus, his entire job centered around something that terrified her. That couldn't be good for a relationship, right?

The guest lodge proudly displayed the legacy of the Cross family. Giant logs wrapped around it, and the natural stone made the mountains beyond the ranch seem like an extension of the lodge itself. In the acreage that spread west from the lodge, Hereford steer stood still in the patchy snow.

He drove the SUV to the back of the property, where the

rec center and smaller cabins were spread out, the space designated for the nonprofit for veterans and their families. Wyoming might be miserably cold at times, but Tripp had learned over the last week that Four Cross Ranch offered its guests plenty of indoor activities to keep busy. Where some Wyoming resorts closed down for the winter, the Crosses kept the fires going for whoever wanted to visit year-round.

He parked, and Cora got out of the SUV. She wobbled, but caught her balance while handling her backpack.

"Whoa, hang on," he said, freeing a strap that had gotten tangled on itself.

"I've got to get to Lexi," she murmured.

"While you do that, I'm going to take Rain back to my cabin."

Her body stiffened, and she glanced to the back of his vehicle. It seemed like she had forgotten about his dog.

Tripp shook his head and tried to hide his grin. She truly lived in her current moment, forgetting all situational awareness. He believed her earlier when she said she didn't see things coming.

She licked her lips. "Will she, um—"

"She won't pay one bit of attention to you unless I tell her to." Tripp squeezed her arm. "But I can also teach you how to tell her it's okay to approach you."

Cora's pretty hazel eyes rounded, and Tripp offered a small smile. "But let's save that for another day," he said gently.

Relief crossed her face, but it didn't last long. She took one long gaze around the neighborhood of small cabins, stopping to study a specific spot of the fence line that butted up against some trees. Her eyes glazed over, but no tears fell.

"Cora?"

"It happened over there," she whispered.

She was no longer in the present. Staring at the spot on the fence line, she'd transported herself backward in time.

He ran the back of his hand down her arm to try and pull her back to the present. "How about I leave Rain in the car for a few minutes while I escort you to Chase and Lexi's cabin?"

"What would happen," she murmured to the spot, "if someone or something attacked you when Rain was around?"

"It wouldn't go well for the attacker."

"Because of Rain? Or because of you?"

"Both."

Her eyes sparked back to the present moment, and she looked to him. "Then let's bring Rain."

Good. She was starting to trust him. Or his dog. Either way, he counted it as a win. Maybe by the time he left town, she would be a bit more comfortable around dogs.

That should make him feel better. Wasn't that part of his job? To help others find their footing around animals through education, training, and practice. Then why was that not enough this time around? Why was that not enough with Cora?

It's not like he could stay in town for forever.

She headed in the direction of Chase and Lexi's home. Newly constructed and serving as their permanent residence, the cabin was larger than the others. And it was a home that would include one tiny additional occupant very soon.

He opened the back of his SUV, as well as the crate inside, and signaled for Rain to exit the vehicle.

Rain obeyed his command and once on the ground, she

shook off the car ride. She took a quick glance at her surroundings and looked to him expectantly.

He reached in his pocket for a treat and slipped it to her. After a good rubdown, he said to her, "Work."

Tripp began walking in Cora's direction, Rain alert at his side. "Heel," he told Rain, and she stepped next to him and stayed close as they approached Cora's slower, clunky, one-booted walk.

Once they caught up to Cora, he and Rain stayed behind her, matching her pace.

Across an open lawn, three families were creating pitiful snowmen with the sparse snow. From the laughter that rang through the air, the families didn't seem to care that their snowmen were short in stature.

This year's winter had been a dry one, though he'd heard reports that was going to change soon.

A woman standing next to a cooler looked familiar. She poured something from a large thermos and handed it to a child.

Another little boy ran across the field and caught his attention.

Waving his gloved hands in the air, and pumping his little legs for all they were worth, four-year-old Cody Wallace bounded toward them. Tripp continued to enjoy his lessons with the boy and training him to work with his new therapy dog.

Cora looked from the boy to Rain and back again. She shuffled to stand in front of Tripp—no, in front of Rain—and her entire body locked tight.

"Heel," Tripp said quietly while keeping his smile on his face for Cody. And for Cora.

Rain's pricked ears stood fully upright, as the canine was anticipating the fun that Cody always brought.

But Cora had frozen in place. "The dog," she whispered.

"It's okay," Tripp said soothingly, stepping beside her. "Rain's highly trained to be around children. But I've worked with Cody several days in the last week. I'm hoping he also remembers what I've taught him."

She looked to him and asked in a surprised tone, "Cody's the one receiving the therapy dog?"

He nodded, not taking his eyes off the boy. "The entire family needs the therapy dog after what happened on the father's last deployment, but technically, Shasta is Cody's. It gives him something good to focus on instead of the things he can't control."

And there were a lot of things that little boy couldn't control in his household with his father's healing injuries both inside and out.

The four-year-old looked like a small, light blue, abominable snowman in his puffer winter jumpsuit and jacket. He came to a skidding halt two feet from Rain.

"Good job, Cody," Tripp said.

"I remembaw," he said. "I remembaw all the things you tol' me."

"Cody, this is my friend Cora. Why don't you show her what we worked on when you approach a dog who isn't yours."

Cody's earnest face looked to Cora. "You have to aks an owner if you can pet their dog."

"Is that right?" Cora said in a tone that made Tripp look to her.

It wasn't just babies. Apparently interacting with any child morphed Cora into a gentle woman capable, if the look on Cody's face told the story, of roping anyone's heart.

Tripp knew how the kid felt. If he wasn't careful, this

woman's bravery was going to suck him in. And he wasn't entirely sure he cared.

Cody cocked his head and asked Cora, "Did you aks Mr. Blackburn if you could play with his dog?"

"Well," she said with a playful tone, "I didn't ask because I'm scared of dogs."

Surprise shot across the kid's face. "Me, too!"

Cora nodded in solemn solidarity.

"My dad was hurt by a dog when he was in the army," he said.

A sheen of moisture covered her eyes. "I'm so sorry, Cody." She paused, looked to Tripp, then back to Cody. "I was hurt by a dog, too. A wolf, actually"

She pulled her hair back for Cody to see. The little boy stood on tiptoes and studied her scars.

Tripp's throat clogged with emotion as he watched Cora's vulnerability.

"Did it hurt?" Cody asked her.

"Yes."

"Was there a lot of blood?"

"Yes."

"And that's why you're scared?"

She nodded.

"It's okay, Miss Cora," Cody said. "You just take it one dog at a time."

Cora's lips parted, but no words came out. She now looked at the boy with the same awe Tripp had felt for her earlier.

Finished doling out sage advice, Cody turned to Tripp. "Mr. Blackburn, may I please play with Rain now?"

Tripp kneeled to Rain and gave her a treat. He walked to Cody and ran his hand through the air from Cody's knees to the ground. "Play."

Immediately, Rain's tail wagged, and she waited for Cody. "Have at it, kid," he said.

Cody bounded to Rain and hugged her around the neck. He released the dog and went running. "Come on, Rain!" His dog caught up to the little boy and she nudged him playfully in the back. Cody's giggles filled the chilled air.

Cora stood and covered her mouth with a hand. "She's just playing."

"She's just playing," Tripp confirmed gently.

"And she doesn't care that I'm standing here."

"She cares. But she's obeying the command I gave her."

Cora watched the dog and boy roll on the ground. "She's amazing," she whispered.

His Labrador retriever had served in many capacities over the years for his clients. She'd been an example of a therapy dog and a service dog for those who had lost hope, she'd helped little ones understand how to interact with animals they didn't know, she'd shown playfulness to soldiers at home who needed to know something existed outside of the military zone, and she'd done an excellent job taking care of Tripp's heart. But in this moment, Tripp couldn't think of a time when he'd been prouder of Rain.

Rain, who could lavish love on Cody with her tongue out and tail wagging. And Rain, who could lavish love on Cora by honoring her boundary.

Cora didn't know who had stolen her heart more. Rain, who knew how to gently roughhouse with a four-year-old boy. Cody, who had conquered his fear. Or Tripp, who had helped Cody conquer that fear.

While the boy played with Rain, Tripp looked at her. "I think you're the one who's amazing."

She blinked. Where had that come from? "What?" she asked.

"You stepped in front of Rain with every intention to protect that boy from my dog."

"I didn't—"

He placed a hand on her arm and squeezed. "You shifted yourself to stand in front of Rain and me, and were ready to defend him."

She looked from Tripp to the spot where she'd stood a few minutes ago and replayed the scene in her head. Realization pulsed from her head all the way down to her cold toes. A smile broke out over her face, one she knew probably looked goofy and proud, but one she couldn't control even if she wanted.

"I did," she whispered.

"You did. You're the bravest person I know," he whispered back. He stepped closer, took a lock of her hair, and folded it around her ear, exposing her scars. Her nerves skittered the way they always did when her scars were out in the open. But maybe they also skittered because of Tripp's touch.

Her scar was private. A hidden battle wound that made some shrink back at the sight of it. An angry, raised, red reminder of a painful day. But Tripp was different. He studied the mark of the wolf with a look of awe. Of respect. And something else she couldn't quite define. He studied it in a way that made her feel safe, a way that made her want to move toward him. Maybe let him take a better look. At it. At her.

For a second, Tripp seemed too close. Or maybe not close enough.

What was it about this man? This man who saw her

and didn't shy away? This man who was amused with her quirks, honored her fears, and made her laugh.

Despite the frigid temperature, warmth spread through her.

In the distance, she could see Chase exiting his cabin. His demeanor seemed relaxed, so all must be well with Lexi at the moment. He confirmed this when he approached them and said, "Lexi's sleeping, so there's no rush to get in there. She left me with instructions to get her a milkshake from the ranch chow hall. I'm headed down there to grab one so it's waiting for her when she wakes."

"Good man," Cora said.

"I learned to survive in the military. It seems to be paying off here with my pregnant wife." He winked at Cora, gave Tripp a pound on the back, and headed down the path.

"That sounds rough," Tripp said to Cora.

"Don't fall for it for one second. Chase loves doting on his wife. He's so excited about this baby, he'd get her one hundred milkshakes if he had to."

The news that Lexi was napping allowed the storm in Cora to calm. She wasn't needed. Yet.

Without her crutches, her boot thudded down the path, and she was thankful she wasn't navigating her way through snow or ice. Otherwise, the lack of precipitation felt disconcerting. They'd had a dry winter. It's like someone forgot to tell Wyoming to turn on the snow.

But that might change next week.

Interrupting her thoughts, Tripp stepped back and looked over the field, and his body immediately went rigid.

When Cora saw what had spooked Tripp, she smiled. As Tripp's half sister approached them, Cora said, "How can you handle the emotions of a soldier with PTSD, but you can't handle a pregnant woman?"

His face turned to granite. "She's out in the cold. Should she be out in temperatures this low?"

Haley couldn't be more bundled for the weather in her jeans, sturdy hiking boots, and durable, navy blue parka. The gloves and hat might even be overkill. "She's just pregnant, Tripp."

"If you say so," he said under his breath.

Haley made it to them, shoved her hands in her coat pockets, and quietly said, "Hey."

"What are you doing out in the cold?" Tripp asked in what could only be described as a protective big-brother tone.

In a quintessential defensive little-sister move, Haley put her hands on her hips. "I work here."

He scratched his head. "Chase said something about that at the hospital. I guess it didn't quite register with everything else going on." A little deflated, Tripp asked, "You work here? At the ranch? What does that mean?"

If Tripp could help Cody, and apparently Cora, conquer her fears, she could return the favor and help smooth things over in his tenuous relationship with his half sister.

Cora interjected, "It's a great opportunity for her to learn the business of the resort."

He studied his half sister. "Why's it a good opportunity?"

Haley shrugged. "I'm studying hotel and restaurant management."

The news seemed to draw Tripp's good attitude back, and he softened his voice. "You're taking college classes?"

"Yes."

"Well, that's—" He scratched his cheek. "That's impressive."

Haley's smile lit up her face. The same smile Cora had

seen on Tripp's face. Cora wondered if the half siblings knew just how deep their similarities ran. Both loyal. Both passionate about what they did. Both with a set of crystal-blue eyes that held stories within their depths. If only these two could find common ground again.

Behind them, Chase scooted past. He held up his wife's milkshake in a short greeting and strode to his house, a man on a mission to return to his very pregnant wife.

While Cora and Haley nodded to Chase as he passed, Tripp studied Haley. "How did you find Four Cross Ranch?" he asked.

"When I still lived in Colorado Springs, I was taking a class at the community college. I met a girl who lived on the old Carson Ranch."

Tripp's eyebrows drew down in confusion, and he cocked his head. "The Carsons didn't have any daughters."

"No," Haley said, "they sold the ranch. And it got turned into a huge home for young women who aged out of the foster-care system, but still needed help starting their adult lives."

"Oh, wow. That's great. Is that old boardinghouse finally being put to good use?"

"Yes. The new owners gutted it and restructured the entire building. My friend lived on the ranch and went through their program." Haley looked down, tapping her toe twice on the ground. "When I found out I was pregnant, my dad was pretty useless. The new owner has a connection to someone who knew Chase from his military days. They called up here and made arrangements for me. It was a fresh start."

Tripp stared at Haley, but he looked lost. As if he wasn't really seeing her. Wherever he was, it wasn't in the present. And by the way his face contorted, it also wasn't a pleasant place to be.

Cora knew Haley didn't share her story with many people. She wanted Tripp to respond to his half sister, to honor her vulnerability. But he hadn't quite pulled himself out of the past.

She stepped toward Haley. Gently, she put her hand through the crook of the other woman's elbow. Quietly, to coax Tripp back into the conversation, she said, "Most of the resorts around here close down for the winter, but Four Cross keeps their doors open all year."

Tripp looked to her, then to Haley. "Is that right?" he asked.

Haley nodded. "I'll eventually get trained on all the major jobs around the resort and the nonprofit. Right now, I plan the on-property activities and coordinate any excursions off-property."

"Do you like your job?" Tripp asked, and Cora wanted to cheer. He still looked uncomfortable with his shifting from side to side, but he was making an effort. And it seemed like Haley was relaxing into their conversation as well.

"For sure," his half sister replied with enthusiasm. "So far, I like this rotation the best. I get to work directly with the families to create a plan catered just for them. Then I set everything in motion and sometimes I even get to join their family activities. It's fun to be a part of something."

"That must be why I haven't seen you around when I'm on the property," he murmured.

When she glanced to Tripp, his eyes seemed to hold the same need. Connection. Family.

But then he caught Cora staring at him, and she felt exposed. Heat hit her face. Maybe *she* was the one who missed connection. It was one thing for her to deliver babies and participate in one of the biggest moments of her patients' lives. It was something completely different to look for that kind of connection for herself.

"Miss Haley, Miss Haley!" Cody called. With a scrunched-up face, the boy rushed to the young woman and threw his arms around her legs.

Rain also hustled to the group. Tripp let out a sharp, quick whistle and held his hand out to Rain, who immediately sat on her back legs next to her owner. Her ears perked, tongue wagged, and she took in each person.

Haley crouched down to eye level with Cody. "Hey, buddy. Your mom wanted me to check on you."

"I'm playing with Rain."

Haley held her palm up high, pulled it down to look at it, then showed her hand to Cody. "But it's not raining, silly boy."

"Not rain from the sky," the little boy said, clearly astounded by her mistake. Then he chuckled, his chubby cheeks full of a smile. "I'm playing with Rain the puppy dog, Miss Haley."

She bopped herself on her forehead and said, "Oh! Rain the puppy dog!"

Cora enjoyed watching the two interact, but glanced at Tripp. He stood stock-still and stared at his little sister. The look on his face held respect.

"We're about to start our game of Bingo," Haley told Cody. "You ready to head inside?"

"What's Bingo?"

Haley sang the Bingo song about the farmer who had a dog, and when she got to the part to spell out the word *Bingo*, Tripp chimed in with her. Quietly at first, then, when Haley looked to him, their volume increased, and their smiles crossed the invisible line between them. Haley stood on the final words, Tripp stepped toward her, and they both leaned toward each other and sang loudly, "And Bingo was his name-o!"

And then, they laughed. As if no one around them existed. The laughter was deep and genuine, and held hope.

"You liked to drive me nuts singing that song when you were little," Tripp said.

"I only sang that song so you would chime in with me. As I recall, if you had just given in and joined me the first time, I wouldn't have sung it so many times in a row."

They grinned at each other, the two of them locked in a happy memory.

Then Tripp sighed. A good, long sigh that released something so that his shoulders lowered just a touch. "You're going to make a great mother, Haley."

A sheen of moisture welled up in Haley's eyes, and she whispered to her half brother, "You think so?"

He squeezed her on the elbow. "I know so."

Cody tugged on Haley's jeans. "Miss Haley, I have to go potty."

She looked down to him. "Okay, buddy. Let's get that taken care of before the game starts."

Haley waved to Tripp, then she and Cody walked across the field hand in hand.

"Well done, Tripp," Cora said softly.

Not taking his eyes off Haley, he nodded. "It's going to be okay."

"Yes. It's going to be very okay," she said.

He turned to her. "How do you feel about heading to Lexi and Chase's now?"

She looked at the courageous little boy who hadn't stopped chattering since he'd walked away from them with

Haley. Then she looked at Rain, who studiously waited for her next direction from her owner. And finally, she studied the place in the forest line that had started her nightmares so many years ago.

But somehow, that place didn't hold as much power as it had the day before.

She smiled at Tripp. "I feel like it's going to be okay."

Chapter Seven

Maybe he could do this.

Maybe Tripp could be a good brother to Haley.

"What?" Cora maneuvered at a steady pace toward Chase and Lexi's house. Two stories of logs fortified the cabin, while stone accents framed one end of the house and chimney. The property edged the line of the forest and faced the smaller cabins. Set apart enough to have privacy, but very clearly still part of the community.

She stopped short of the porch and angled her body to him. "What did you say?"

Had he said his thoughts out loud? Never one to blush, Tripp still couldn't deny the heat that hit his face. Rain came to a halt at his side and butted up against his left hand, almost as if she was giving him courage. "I said, maybe I can do this."

"Do what?"

He shrugged. "Be a big brother to Haley. Be a good uncle to her baby."

She searched his face. He didn't know what she was looking for, but he sure hoped she found it. He was getting attached to being around Cora. It'd been so long since he'd dated, Tripp had forgotten what it was like to care what a woman thought about him.

Cora was different. She wasn't just any woman. She'd seen his struggle with Haley and helped him in spite of himself. With her by his side, he felt a little bit invincible.

A smile broke across her face. "I think you could be a wonderful big brother to Haley."

There it was again. That confidence she had in him that made him feel like he'd won Best in Show.

"Speaking on behalf of all little sisters," she said, "big brothers are important."

He thought of Chase's affection for Cora. Hunter's protectiveness. Even the never-seen younger brother Ryder seemed to have a hold on Cora, though his was more like a peer she respected. Suddenly, Tripp wanted all those things for Haley. He wanted to *be* all those things for Haley. And much more.

"You going to help me learn to be a good big brother?" he asked.

"Absolutely." She looked down to her boot, then back up to him, and stared at him from under her long, dark eyelashes. "Does that mean that you might come around here more often?" she asked softly. Almost bashfully. Definitely with vulnerability.

Vulnerability looked good on Cora. It was something she didn't show many people, and that was a gift to him. Something he hoped he never took for granted. And something, he only now realized, he wanted to see more of in the future.

He took a step closer to her.

The soft wind blew a lock of hair into her face. He lifted his hand and ran two fingers across her cheek, catching the piece and skimming her scars to curl it around her ear. "I can think of other things that might cause me to come around here more often."

She blinked. Then lifted her face to him, her eyes locked on his.

He leaned in, feeling an undeniable draw to Cora. A draw he'd felt since the first time she stepped in front him at the diner.

But the creak of the cabin door quickly ended the moment.

Tripp jumped back and shoved his hands in his jeans pockets. Cora moved to face Chase, who stood on the porch, arms crossed over his chest. Even Rain stood at attention as if she, too, understood the meaning of the assessing gaze of Cora's big brother.

"Everything okay out here?" Chase asked in a tone that communicated there wasn't a right answer to the question.

Oh, boy. Firsthand experience with a protective brother. Tripp wanted to learn how to *be* that kind of a brother. He had no interest in being on the receiving end of that kind of a brother.

"Everything's fine," Cora said in a practiced little-sister tone that, while calmly stated, implied a swift kick to her brother to stay out of her business.

Chase's face said the current situation was everything *but* fine. "Do I need to send Tripp to work on the fence?"

"If Tripp earns a reason to work on the fence, I'll send him there myself."

"Work on the fence?" he murmured out of the side of his mouth to Cora.

She lowered her voice and turned her head slightly to him while maintaining eye contact with her brother. "Anytime one of us had a bad attitude or disobeyed, Mom and Dad sent us to work on the fence. No matter how young. With so many acres of land, different pastures, and animals at the ready to break the fence line, it's a miserable, never-ending, hard-labor job."

"Sounds awful."

"When boys started paying attention to me, Dad, then later Hunter, sent them to the fence line before they could even talk to me."

He grimaced. "That's rough."

"You have no idea. " She returned her attention to Chase "So he's not going to work on the fence."

"That's a shame," Chase responded. "Lexi just sent me to work on the fence. So it's no problem to take Tripp along with me."

"I have no idea what you did, but you probably deserve it," Cora said, goading her brother. "Is Lexi awake?"

"I see what you're doing. You think you can distract me with my pregnant wife?"

She thudded up the stairs past Chase and paused at the front door. "I absolutely know I can distract you with your pregnant wife."

With one final glare at Tripp, Chase asked, "You coming in?"

Tripp took the porch steps porch two at a time and followed Chase into the front room.

Upon entry, Rain went on alert, panting, tail wagging.

Once Tripp's eyes adjusted to the lighting, he saw why.

Lexi was lying sprawled across the couch, her hand on the head of their golden retriever, the dog's head on her pregnant belly.

And Cora was on the other side of the room from Lexi, frozen in place.

Quickly, Tripp swiped his hand down to signal Rain to stay. Not entirely pleased with this command, his dog glanced rapidly back and forth between her fellow canine and her owner.

"I know, girl. Hang on," he said in a low voice.

Lexi surveyed the room, and when she noticed Cora, she said to her husband, "Chase, you should have put Duke in our bedroom before your sister came inside."

Regret crossed Chase's face. "I'm sorry, Cora. I wasn't thinking. But Duke barely pays attention to anyone else. He hasn't left Lexi's side since she became pregnant."

Lexi rubbed Duke's head, looking at her dog with all the affection in the world, but speaking to everyone in the room. "I think he knew I was pregnant before I knew."

"It's possible," Tripp said, fascinated with Duke's position on her belly. "Some dogs can sense hormonal shifts."

Slowly, Tripp sidestepped to Cora, but asked Lexi, "Anything changed in his attention on you recently?"

When he reached Cora, without calling attention to his movements, he took her cold hand in his. She squeezed. Hard.

"Well," Lexi said on a sigh, "two days ago he started to do exactly what you're seeing. Anytime I sit where my stomach is available to him, he gently rests his head on top of it."

Tripp rubbed his thumb down each of Cora's fingers, soothing her grip with each run down her knuckles.

"How are your contractions?" When he asked Lexi this question, Cora's torso jerked, as if she had abruptly returned to the conversation in the room. Her sixth sense about pregnant women had kicked into place.

But Tripp's question seemed to spark annoyance from Lexi. "Just Braxton Hicks. But I'm going on record now to say that if one more person tells me this baby isn't coming anytime soon, I'm going to knock them off their rocker and not feel bad about it at *all*."

Chase moved toward her and calmly asked, "Honey, would you like your milkshake now?"

His wife shot daggers at Chase. "Do you mean do I want my *vanilla* shake now? As opposed to the chocolate one that I always crave?"

Chase looked over at them and said sheepishly, "The wrong shake flavor gets you sent to the fence."

Duke lifted his head, becoming alert, and sent what could only be described as a judgmental look at Chase. Even his dog knew Chase had broken the rules.

Lexi looked to Cora and threw her hands out in disgust. "Who gets a pregnant woman a vanilla shake? Vanilla is the most useless flavor on the planet. At best, it shines as a complement to other desserts. A splash of vanilla in a batch of cookies. A side of vanilla ice cream with some apple pie. But it's not the main event. It's not the Show. It's not the Super Bowl."

"Honey, you know I don't do sports analogies," Chase said.

Tripp knew Lexi was just about to throttle her husband. Even Duke growled at Chase, which he figured stressed Cora even more than she already was.

But then, Rain broke command, and sat five feet in front of Cora on alert. Ready to protect her.

Tripp stood still, unable to process what he'd just seen from his highly trained, impeccably behaved, always obedient dog.

Cora whispered, "Did Rain just..."

"Yeah," he said. "She's protecting you."

"Even though you told her to—"

"Stay."

He'd have to deal with that later. Technically, Rain was doing what he wanted her to do. He wanted her to protect Cora. Tripp shook his head and turned his body to shield Cora from the room but kept her hand in his. "Duke's growling because he knows Lexi's upset at Chase. She's safe. And you're safe because Rain has decided you're hers to protect even if that means disobeying orders."

"Lexi might be safe from that dog, but my brother is being a complete idiot. She's going to kill him if his dog doesn't first."

There she was.

Tripp breathed a little easier.

"The woman clearly needs chocolate," he said in a low voice. "Let's go get her the correct shake."

"I'm here to check on Lexi."

"If Lexi hasn't had any contractions, she's not in labor, right?"

"Right."

"But her dog clearly homed in on something. Like I said, research says that some dogs can sense hormonal changes in pregnant women. Which tells me that she'll probably deliver soon, but with no contractions, it's not immediate." He squeezed her hand. "So we have time to go get that shake, find our footing a little, and let Chase take care of Duke while we're gone."

She shifted her gaze down and to the side and let out a long sigh. When she looked back to him, he saw resignation in her eyes, but he could also feel the relief coming off her body. "Are you trying to take my job?" she asked.

"Not on your life. The second your sister-in-law has a contraction, I'm out. My knowledge about pregnant women will have maxed out."

"Okay." She straightened her shoulders, let go of his

hand, and hobbled a step around him. "Chase, I'm going to save your hide just like I did when we were kids."

Clearly not agreeing with his little sister's assessment of their childhood, Chase opened his mouth, but Cora wouldn't let him get a word in edgewise.

"We're headed to grab Lexi a chocolate shake, as well as three extra shakes, because if the storm they keep talking about actually hits, you don't want to get caught chocolate-shake-free."

"Clearly, this woman is a professional," Lexi chided Chase.

Cora plodded out of the house, Rain giving her five feet of distance from all angles, but always placing her body between Cora and Duke.

When Tripp thought Cora was out of hearing distance, he said in a low voice, "Maybe when we return, you could put Duke in another room while Cora talks to Lexi." It wasn't a question. It wasn't a command. But it also wasn't a request. He meant every word. For Cora.

Chase's sharp, judgmental eyes, which had been focused on Tripp earlier, relaxed. The other man seemed to be looking at him with something that felt a lot like respect. As if Tripp had passed some big-brother test. An important one.

"We'll take care of it," Chase said just before he dropped to his knees, kissed Lexi on the forehead, and murmured something to her. It was as if they were the only two people in the room along with their love for each other and the anticipation of what was to come.

And Tripp was caught. Maybe this is something he wanted for himself someday. Maybe his future could hold more than just being a good brother to Haley, and a good uncle to his niece or nephew. Maybe he could eventually have his own family and his own glowing pregnant wife who had crazy cravings he wouldn't be able to keep up with.

He wondered what Cora would think about all of those maybes.

"Well, what do you think?" Lexi asked after Cora's exam and assessment, a small crease of concern etched in her forehead.

"I think you are perfectly healthy." Cora offered an encouraging smile. "Everything looks good to me."

After a sip of her shake, Lexi said, "I'm not going into labor anytime soon, am I? No, wait." She held up a hand. "Don't tell me. It will just depress me. It feels like I'm going to spend eternity on this couch and if your answer is anything other than 'you're in labor and about to give birth,' I'm not sure I can handle it."

Cora perched on the side of the couch. "I will say, I never thought I'd see the day where I'd agree with a dog's medical assessment, but I think Duke's right. Things have shifted, as we have discussed. You are getting closer."

Lexi ran her hands over her belly and smiled at the bump, then she frowned and looked to Cora. "I'm sorry about Duke earlier. I don't know your story, Cora. Chase once said that was yours to tell. But I know something happened, and that we should have done a better job keeping Duke in the next room. I'm sorry."

Cora reached for the blood-pressure cuff on the coffee table and slowly wrapped the long black tubing around the Velcro armband. "It's okay. It was a long time ago."

Lexi cocked her head to the side. "It seems you have someone who's pretty protective of you these days."

Heat hit Cora's face and she bent to pack the cuff in

her backpack, hoping to buy some time so the blush that she knew had crept over her face would go back where it belonged. Hidden.

While she fiddled with the zipper on the pack, Lexi placed her hand on Cora's arm. "I didn't mean to embarrass you. Sometimes I just…well, sometimes I just wonder if you need a girlfriend to talk to."

All Cora could do was blink.

"You're stuck with all these Cross men, who love you dearly and mean well, but probably don't always know what to say or how to say it." When their chuckles died down, with a softer tone she continued, "And you've got so many women you mentor through pregnancy, childbirth, and beyond, but I don't get the sense that you're close to any of them."

Cora gathered her hands in her lap and looked down while Lexi finished. "And our situations aren't the same, but I know what it's like to wish you had a mom you could confide in."

That's when something speared Cora in the heart.

Whether it was the open wound from the death of her parents that never seemed to heal, or acknowledging that she wished she had her mother at a time like this, she knew what that pain meant.

She needed to talk to someone.

Honestly, she was relieved Lexi opened the door to this conversation because she had no idea how to handle her feelings.

Finally, she looked to her sister-in-law. "I think I like him," she whispered.

"Why do you say it like it's a bad thing?" Lexi asked, then gave Cora a smile full of understanding, giddiness, and gentle amusement.

Leaning back from the couch, Cora craned her neck to try to see or hear the men. When the coast seemed to be clear, she said, "He lives in Colorado."

"Chase said Tripp stayed in Elk Run to help you. And where he lives is just geography. That can change."

Sweat broke out on her forehead. "Do you know what he does for a living? His whole life centers around dogs. I'm terrified of them."

Lexi took a breath and said, "He seemed to be very in-tune to your needs around Rain and Duke. Very protective—" she poked Cora in the arm "—of you."

Flustered feelings swirled around Cora like an encroaching storm. She wiped her forehead with her sleeve. "With my job, I don't know how to date. It's all about the mommas and the babies for me. Who wants to marry a person who has one foot out the door every time she's needed for a delivery?"

"Are you the only midwife in the state of Wyoming?"

Exasperated, Cora threw out her hands. "Can we go back to just being sisters-in-law? This girlfriend-advice thing isn't going so well for me."

The women looked at each other, paused, then burst out laughing. When they quieted down, Lexi said gently, "You seem to be taking a chance on dogs just by being around Rain. I wonder what it would be like for you to take a chance with more humans, ones that aren't babies."

Tears welled up in Cora's eyes. "I don't want any more scars," she whispered.

"I know."

"But I also don't want to be scared anymore," she added.

A kind smile broke over Lexi's face. "I think there's a man and his dog who would be so happy to know that."

Cora picked up her backpack to put it on her lap. "Now,

why would you say that? You haven't been around us that long."

Us. Cora heard her own word before the knowing look showed on Lexi's face.

"It doesn't take long to see that both man and dog are quite fond of you."

Cora pushed to stand, balancing on her nonbooted foot while she slung her backpack over her shoulders. "I think the pregnancy hormones are starting to get to you."

"Probably," Lexi said when Cora leaned down to hug her, "but that doesn't mean I'm wrong."

The crisp air felt good in Cora's lungs. Then again, the ranch air always did that for her. But it had been years since she'd felt the freedom in the fresh air.

After the attack, all the oxygen on the property seemed to be sucked up by the stitches on her face, the fear coursing through her veins, and the thick burden of guilt Hunter wore when he was around her.

But today was different. Today was lovely, safe, and beautiful. And it might just be because of a man named Tripp, a boy named Cody, and, ironically, a dog named Rain.

After the correctly flavored shake had been successfully delivered to Lexi, Tripp and Cora walked in comfortable silence down a newly laid path that led to the chow house. Lexi and the baby were just fine. Chase would hover over his wife until the baby came, but he looked a little more at peace when she left their cabin.

Cora surveyed the land and trees around her. "It feels odd for this place not to be covered in snow."

"Chase said that the weatherman predicts a nice-sized snowstorm is coming."

"You never can predict what's going to come off the mountains around here. Chase knows that. Sometimes the forecasts are correct, but other times the mountains will stop a storm in its tracks, or the wind shifts those big storms right out of the way. I think it's a job requirement for a Wyoming weather man to know how to apologize when the storm doesn't land the way they said it would."

"I'm not sure this one is going away."

She stopped and looked up at him, Tripp stopping as well, with Rain at his far side. "When's it supposed to hit?" she asked in her tone that said, "I prepare for worst-case scenarios because I am responsible for tiny humans."

"A week," he said.

"We're going to have to think about contingency plans. I have too many pregnant mommas close to delivery who I'll need to be able to help."

Tripp rubbed his jaw with the back of his hand. "That won't be easy with families living across three counties."

He would know. He'd been her chauffeur for two weeks now. Something he didn't mind nearly as much as he thought he would.

Which made her wonder what the next two weeks might hold, filling her stomach with butterflies. He said he might come around more often, and not just for his future nephew.

"Cora, did you hear me?" Tripp asked, then she looked at him questioningly.

"Where did you go just now?"

Her face filled with heat, and she knew she must be blushing.

A smile tugged at the corners of his mouth and his eyes bore into hers as if he knew exactly where her thoughts had been just now.

She cleared her throat and began walking again. "I lost my train of thought and missed what you said. Could you repeat it, please?"

"I said, 'Is there room on the ranch for the families?'"

She stopped walking again. "Room on the ranch for what?"

"Boy, you really lost track of our conversation, didn't you?" A slow smile curved his mouth. "I might pay money to know what distracted you."

Ignoring the second round of butterflies floating through her belly, she fake-glared at him. "Stay on task. Room on the ranch for what?"

"If the weather stays true to the forecast, and there's room on the ranch, maybe we should convince your pregnant mommas to bring their families to stay here for a few days. Just in case."

She looked at him, surprised. "Tripp, that's brilliant."

He cocked an eyebrow. "It was brilliant the first time I said it, too."

Giggling, she said, "Stop giving me a hard time."

When they started walking again, he murmured, "Maybe someday you'll tell me what you were thinking about."

"Right now, I'm thinking about the logistics of your idea. There might be some cabins available from the non-profit that could hold individual families. But they're spread too far apart across the property for me to take care of everyone at the same time. I'm not snowshoe ready," she said, pointing down to the medical boot.

"What about the lodge?"

"If it has availability, that would be ideal, having everyone in the same place. I'll reach out to Chase and ask."

She looked out over the ranch. "And then we can pray not everyone goes into labor at the same time."

The color drained from Tripp's face. "Is that a possibility?" His voice almost squeaked with the question.

"Don't worry—" she patted him on the arm "—if I need help, I'll talk you through it."

She left him standing there stunned as she continued down the path toward the SUV.

"That's not what I signed up for." She heard him say it from behind her. Then louder the second time as he hurried his steps to catch up to her. "Cora, I'm your driver. I know dogs. Not babies."

Turnabout was fair play. Continuing to goad him, she said when he caught up to her, "Babies don't wait, Tripp. Low-pressure systems can put moms into labor. They're called Storm Babies." He gasped, and she continued. "Besides, I'm sure you've helped deliver a puppy or two, right? Not much different."

Stopping dead in his tracks while she continued on, incensed, he called after her, "Not much different? There's plenty different…"

Unable to help herself, she threw her head back and laughed.

When he caught up to her, he shook his head. "Now, you're just messing with me."

"Storm Babies are a real thing, but yeah, I'm messing with you just a little bit."

He sighed, smiling. "Well played, Cora. Well played."

"I might need your help, but I promise to keep it to tasks you're comfortable with. And if we're really doing this, I'll ask Haley if she can stay at the lodge as well."

"Haley? Why would you ask Haley?"

Cora gentled her voice. "She's not a kid anymore, Tripp."

"I'm starting to understand that."

"Plus, she knows the women in the expectant-moms group. There's mutual respect among them. It's a safe space, which allows them to help each other."

He confessed, "Learning to think of her as an adult is harder than I imagined."

She looked at him and said in all seriousness, "If we do this, I need you trust that *I* know what I'm doing. Don't second-guess anything I might ask her or you to do. Just do it."

One of her gloves sat twisted on her hand. Trying to fix it while walking, she lost her balance on her new boot and wobbled, only for Tripp to steady her at her elbow.

He felt a little too close, so much so that those butter-flies ignited in her stomach again.

His voice lowered, and he said, "If it's one thing I've learned in the last couple of weeks, Cora, it's that you know exactly what you're doing. And you do it with an uncommon courage."

He lifted a hand to her face and gently traced the scar down the side of her cheek. The scar she usually took great pains to cover. The scar that he studied with an open look of reverence.

Almost imperceptibly, he leaned toward her, glancing at her eyes. Then shifted closer.

"Anything I can help you with, Tripp?" A brother's voice. Almost identical to the last time Tripp drew this close to her and they'd been interrupted. But this time, the voice belonged to Hunter.

Everything inside of Cora deflated. All she needed was Ryder to interrupt a moment between them and it would complete the Cross-brothers trifecta ruining her dating life.

Tripp shook his head and turned to Hunter. "Not right now. Thanks, Hunter."

Hunter glared at Tripp for three seconds longer than necessary, then looked to Cora and asked, "Do I need to send Tripp to work the fence line?"

For some reason, this made Tripp chuckle, but Cora didn't find anything funny about her protective brother at all. She crossed her arms. "No. But you can tell me if the lodge is booked up over the next week."

"I'm not sure. Chase keeps track of the calendar. Why?"

"If it's not booked, I'd like to bring in some expectant families to stay here through the bad weather so I can be close in case anyone needs me."

A look of surprise appeared on her brother's usually stoic face as if he'd just realized where she was. "It's been a while since you've been at the ranch," he said in a gruff voice.

She bit back tears. Out of everyone, Hunter understood the most what it cost her to come on the property. "Lexi needed me," she said, and shrugged.

He nodded. "Well, it's good to see you here. I'll check with Chase and get back to you," he said, stalking off before she could say anything else. Before she could address the emotion she thought she heard in his voice.

Hunter had a heart the size of Wyoming. Maybe having protective brothers wasn't always such a bad thing after all.

When she looked back at Tripp, he asked, "Ready to go?"

She took a few steps down the path, but stopped when she realized Tripp and Rain weren't by her side. When she looked back, he was studying her.

"What is it?" she asked.

"Do you have any appointments tomorrow?"

"Nothing on the calendar, unless someone calls me."

He shifted from one foot to the other. "I think we should...go— I think we should..."

Why did he seem nervous?

He looked at the ground, then back to her. "I think we should go to the park," he said finally.

She looked around, confused. "The park?"

"If snow's about to cover us for a few days, we should take advantage of the time before it gets here."

"The park?" She still didn't understand.

"I've got a cooler for food, a space heater, some blankets, and a dog that needs some wide-open space to run."

"That sounds like a picnic," she said. *That sounds like a date*, she almost said out loud. Then she felt her eyes go wide. "The park," she whispered.

His grin spread into a wide, handsome smile. "The park. But don't worry. I won't let it go to your head. We have some work to do."

"We do?"

"Yes. We've got to talk through how to run the lodge if it's available, as well as a contingency plan if there's no space on the ranch."

"So it's a working thing," she said more lightly, nodding. "At the park."

He twirled his keys in his hands. "At the park," he repeated as he passed her.

Chapter Eight

"You're doing it again," Tripp said the next day, listening to Cora's pen rattle against the clipboard he knew was in front of her on the picnic table.

"I'm not doing it again," she replied, clearly still doing it because he could still hear the unrelenting sound.

"I thought the park would be a good idea," he said from where he was sprawled out on top of a blue woolen ranch blanket on the picnic table bench. Arms crossed on his chest. Eyes closed. "I'd eat a hamburger. You'd eat a salad that tasted like cardboard. We'd pin down plans for the next week at the lodge and then relax."

"The park was a great idea. And my salad was far from cardboard."

"We'll have to agree to disagree." He sighed. "I don't think you understand the definition of relaxing."

"We've secured the ranch lodge officially. And now, we're working on the details. I thought the point was to come up with a plan for my patients and the impending weather."

"It was. But now, we're done." The temperature had a small bite to it, but a strong sun in the sky continued to hold off the gray clouds.

"I'm just going over the list."

"Again." He sat up and placed his body directly across from hers. "You're just going over the list *again*."

But she looked cute doing it. No scrubs and Henleys today. Instead, she was wearing a red sweater under her coat and dark jeans. Between her nonwork clothes and his clean shave, the trip to the park felt a little more like a date than the usual carting her around the county to see patients.

"You were also working during this picnic," she said, defending herself as she stared at her notes.

"I had to do a little work. The foster family I thought might back out confirmed that they do, in fact, need to pass on this new litter. I needed to reach out to others who have fostered for me in the past to see if they could lend a hand. I'm still waiting to hear back." He still wasn't sure what he was going to do if he couldn't find anyone.

She looked to him, and her demeanor changed. "I'm sorry," she said softly, with the same tone he'd seen her use with the babies. Soothing. He could get used to the soft touch of her voice.

Which is why he took advantage of the moment and snatched the clipboard right out from under her.

"Hey, wait a second. I might have forgotten—"

"You have forty-two items listed. And you've texted all of the tasks you want to delegate, *and* heard back from everyone with a resounding yes to your requests." He shoved the clipboard underneath the blanket. "Work's over."

She crossed her arms and sighed, looking out over the cold, dry field. "Well. Now what? Is the picnic over?"

He stood, held out a hand for her, and said, "This picnic is definitely not over."

After grabbing a Frisbee out of his backpack, he led her

to the edge of the field, the dead winter grass crackling under their feet. "Wanna play Frisbee with Rain and me?"

She stiffened.

"Or just me?" he said gently. "It's your choice. But let me tell you that there's a way to play Frisbee with Rain where you can throw to her, and I instruct her to bring it to me so you don't have to interact with her."

"And that won't confuse her?"

"No. I do it all the time with clients." He didn't tell her it was to help them get more comfortable with dogs.

Tripp set them up in a triangle and gave Rain the command. Cora's body locked tight when she first threw to Rain, but on the third round, with the dog's run to drop it at Tripp's feet, and his throw back to Cora, she smiled broadly at him.

"I don't remember the last time I threw a Frisbee," she said right before she released the disc in Rain's direction.

The dog shot like a cannon in whatever direction Cora threw, which varied widely with each attempt. Her Frisbee skills felt like a nod to her driving skills. It was probably best that she was throwing to Rain and not to him. He didn't think he could keep up with her erratic aim.

Which he found adorable.

"When do you relax, Cora?"

Her next throw went straight into the ground. Rain was elated with the challenge and flew to try to intercept the bounce.

Cora rested her hands on her hips. "Are you about to lecture me on work-life balance? Because I'm a step ahead of you."

Rain brought the Frisbee over to him. When Tripp took it out of her mouth, the dog had a smile on her face while she was panting.

"You're always a step ahead of me, with or without crutches," he said as he flung the Frisbee to her, "but this time tell me how you're a step ahead of me about relaxation."

She bobbled the catch. "After I almost missed a birth last fall, I started searching for a second midwife to work with me to serve this area."

"Any luck?"

She held the Frisbee close to her chest while she studied Rain. "I found one woman interested in coming out here. We met and hit it off. I need to give her a little time to finish her training. The plan is for her to move here and shadow me for a while, then I can let her loose."

"Do you want a family?" he asked, knowing he was asking a deliberate question.

Alarm crossed her face, then she said quietly, "Yes."

"So having a partner would allow you some freedom to be able to do that." He shrugged. "Someday."

She didn't look away when a smile curved at the edges of her mouth. "Someday," she said. It seemed deliberately.

Studying Rain, she said, "I think I want to pet her. Can I do that without her pouncing on me?" she asked, not taking her eyes off his dog.

Rain looked expectantly between Tripp and Cora, probably waiting on someone to keep the game going, but maybe because she understood Cora's question. At least, that's what Tripp believed about his intuitive dog. She knew something significant was happening.

"I can make that happen." Tripp heard the thickness in his voice and wondered if she did, too. She was brave in every area of her life.

He held out his hand for Rain to stay, then walked to Cora and sat down on the cold ground about three feet from her. With the hand farthest from Cora, he pulled treats out of his jacket pocket and held them out when he called to Rain.

His dog bounded to him, gobbled the treats and, on command, lay down next to Tripp.

He made the same command he did in the diner to tell Rain not to move toward Cora, then looked to Cora.

"She won't come to you."

"Can I—can I sit next to you?"

"Yes," he said. "I'm also going to grab hold of Rain's collar so you're assured that she won't be able to come at you."

Without taking her eyes off Rain, Cora nodded, then slowly moved toward them. Tripp offered her a hand and, very ungracefully, she sat down next to Tripp, tucked her uninjured leg in, and left her booted foot out, creating a triangle between the three of them.

She was much closer to Rain than Tripp ever thought she would get, which only made him prouder of them both. Rain, with her respect and obedience on one side of him, and Cora, with her courage and big heart on his other side.

Cora held out her hand, and Rain sniffed, but stayed very still. Cora lifted her hand and petted the top of Rain's head with the same calm and soothing movements Tripp had seen her use with newborns.

At first, the interaction went well. But after a few moments, Rain jerked her head up and sneezed, causing Cora to rear back and let out a yelp.

Tripp closed his eyes in disappointment. "I'm sorry, Cora. Dogs sneeze, but that was unfortunate timing."

Cora laughed nervously. "Of course. She had to sneeze. Everyone needs to sneeze. That's a normal thing."

He placed his hand over hers and looked at her. "I'm sorry."

"I, um…" She looked out over the field. "I think I'm done for today."

"Hang on," he said. "Just stay here for a second."

Tripp walked Rain over to the picnic table. He grabbed a rawhide out of his backpack that he left for her with the command to stay where she sat. He snagged a blanket and the space heater and carried them to where Cora sat.

Once he spread it over the ground next to her, he helped her move to the top of the blanket, placed the heater between them, and sat down.

Cora might look like she wanted to bolt after her interaction with Rain, but he didn't want their picnic to end on that note. Plus, he'd really enjoyed their time together so far. And he thought she had, too.

There was still so much more that he wanted to know about her.

For a few long minutes, they sat in silence, both looking out over the park. A soft wind blew, bringing whispers of the colder weather to come.

Cora wasn't sure what Tripp was thinking about, but she was trying to run the scene with Rain over in her head. Of course, a dog sneezes. Dogs sneeze. It was even a cute sneeze, Cora could admit. Rain had scrunched up her nose just like a person would, and the sneeze had shaken the dog's body all over. It was simultaneously normal and jarring.

But the fact that Cora voluntarily petted Rain had to count for something, didn't it? And the part where she didn't run screaming from either man or his dog had to be worth even more points.

She wasn't sure, but it felt like maybe she could try to get used to Rain. Become more comfortable around the canine. Around her owner.

That still didn't mean Tripp and Cora were meant to be together. Though, admittedly, if Cora had a second midwife working with her, it opened up a world of possibilities for her. Including more time for a personal life. Still, how would they solve the issue of geography?

Was Tripp thinking about the same things?

"What's up with the bulletin board at your house?" he asked, still staring at the field.

Nope. Definitely not thinking about the same things. Good to know.

"What's wrong with my bulletin board?"

"There aren't any pictures of you with the babies you deliver."

She stayed silent, not knowing how to answer the question without completely exposing herself. Lexi's words came back to her. *You seem to be taking a chance on dogs... I wonder what it would be like for you to take a chance with humans...*

Tripp sat up straight and looked at her, as if something had just dawned on him. "You don't like to be photographed with the babies. You—" he shook his head "—you cover your scars and back away, often offering to take the pictures yourself. Even when they ask you to be in the picture."

She looked away. "You think you're so smart, don't you?"

"I don't have to be a genius to figure you out." He moved to sit in front of her. "I've witnessed you do it several times myself."

"When a baby is born, I shouldn't be the focus in that

moment, Tripp," she said a little defensively. "Everyone is and should be focused on the precious child that just arrived in the world. Whatever happened in the past or is going to happen in the future just fades away when the baby comes."

He looked at her, concentration all over his face as if deciding something. Then he reached over and, as if to give her a choice, slowly curled a piece of hair around her ear, exposing the scars.

After a pause, he reverently ran his fingertips down the length of the marks on her face. She'd never let anyone do that before, and it felt scary, but somehow also safe.

"You let everyone's attention stay on the baby so you can hide your scars," he said gently.

"I'm not the focus, Tripp," she said, her voice wobbling.

His eyes locked onto hers, and he drew forward just a touch. "Maybe you should be," he said. "Just for one picture. To honor your work, your expertise, and your love for that child."

She swallowed, tried to fortify herself, then said the scariest thing she could think of. "No one wants something ugly in the picture with their beautiful new baby."

He looked confused, then hurt, like she'd just slapped him. "You're the most beautiful woman I know," he whispered, and her stomach leaped. "I wish you'd stop hiding."

Her mouth opened, but no words came out.

"Stop hiding behind the babies. Just let people see you." He leaned in, a breath away. "I see you."

He saw her. He saw *her*.

"This doesn't make sense, Tripp. *We* don't make sense."

"Geography. Jobs. Dogs. I can't solve it all right now. But make no mistake, Cora. We're definitely starting to make sense, you and I," he whispered.

Maybe he was thinking about the same things she was earlier.

I don't want to be scarred and scared anymore.

"We might be starting to make sense," she whispered back.

He cupped her cheeks, and his eyes scanned her face. She couldn't breathe. Then he shifted and placed the most gentle, reverent kiss on her cheekbone over what she knew were the tips of her scars.

When he pulled back, they stared at each other. More than geography, jobs, dogs, and scars passed between them. But she still had so many questions.

Then her phone rang abruptly, reminding her of said job, and she took the call to talk to one of the families who would be moving onto the ranch with them when the weather arrived.

Because whether she liked it or not, a storm was coming.

However, instead of braving this storm alone, she would have Tripp by her side. Something that, despite the colder temperatures coming, warmed her heart. And if she went by Tripp's sweet kiss on her cheek, she knew the thought of being by her side warmed his heart, too.

Chapter Nine

Whatever Tripp thought had passed between Cora and him earlier this week was nowhere to be found today. Gone was the sweet, blushing, flirtatious, confident woman.

She'd turned into a task-driven, fury of a woman dead set on protecting all who called her midwife.

Around him, people scurried about the lodge, preparing for the upcoming storm while getting ready to host three pregnant women and their husbands. He caught sight of Cora in the open living room walking toward him.

She pushed the long sleeves of her Henley up her forearms. He avoided telling her that the scrubs that she wore made her look cute. She would not welcome a compliment at that moment, he guessed, but he was hoping she'd accept his support.

"Why aren't the Hortons here yet?" she asked curtly.

"I called them. The lock on their car froze and Ethan poured hot water on it." He looked at her and shrugged because they both knew what that meant. "It refroze the locks."

She looked incredulous. "Why in the world would he do such a thing?"

"Two reasons. He's a Texas transplant and has no clue how to handle his first winter storm. When I talked to him, he said south of the Rio Grande River, everything just shuts down at the first sign of snow. But more importantly," he continued, gentling his voice, "the due date of their first child is approaching, and he's trying to take care of his wife during a winter storm. He's a little nervous."

Her features softened. "He's nervous," she repeated, her tone full of understanding.

"Yeah." He reached out and squeezed her shoulder.

She looked at him. "You doing okay?"

"Great. You?"

She nodded once, glancing around the house. "I think we might just pull this off." Before he could respond, she retreated, leaving him alone with the fading *clud-thunk* of her clog and her medical boot. Again.

He found himself crossing his arms, then uncrossing them, then crossing them again. Okay. He got it. She was in the zone, and he needed to find somewhere else to be helpful.

His phone buzzed, and he pulled it out of the back pocket of his jeans. The caller ID told him it was his breeder. With Tripp still needing one family to foster, he hoped this was good news. He lifted the phone to his ear to take the call, but Cora had returned from down the hall.

When she got close, she furrowed her brow and crossed her arms.

Uh-oh.

He hit the button to send the call to voice mail and lowered the phone. "Everything okay?"

"Why is there a bed and a space heater set up in the downstairs office?"

What could be interpreted as hostility came off Cora in waves. But he knew it was just the stress, coming out sideways and aimed at anything in her path. And right now, that was him. Which was fine. He'd take one for the team.

Slowly, he walked to her, his hands up in surrender. With a soothing voice, he said, "I know we talked about shutting the vents everywhere in the house so we could focus the heat centrally and use the fireplace in the living room. But Karen gets nauseated at the smell of burning firewood—"

"It's been an expensive winter without the fireplace," Dalton, Karen's husband called from the open kitchen. "Each pregnancy, a different smell plagues her the entire nine months. It turns off like clockwork once she delivers. I need this baby to come so I can light the fireplace again and lower our heating bills."

Tripp had learned Dalton and Karen were Wyoming natives and this was going to be their fourth baby. The man seemed a little more relaxed than first-time fathers-to-be Ethan and Chase.

"I bet," Tripp chuckled and exchanged a look with Dalton. Then he glanced back to Cora. "It's all taken care of. Everything has been moved to the office for Karen and it's ready to go."

"Why didn't you let me know?"

"You were handling other stuff. I wanted to take something off your plate."

"But I could have helped."

Any response he gave Cora right now would be tricky. She was already frustrated with how little she could carry because of her healing ankle and the awkward boot.

"Hunter and I took care of it," he said carefully.

"Where is he now?"

"He was going to clean the gutters so when the thaw comes, there's a clear path for the water to drain instead of backing up into the roof. When he finished with that, he was off to help get some cattle moved."

"That sounds like him."

Tripp's phone sounded again, and he glanced at the screen, this time seeing the name *Jenson*, the foster family he was depending on taking four German shepherd pups. He grimaced at the screen. Those two calls close together couldn't be good.

"You seem busy," Cora said, impatience lining her tone.

His gut clenched, and his eyes shot to hers as he shoved his phone in his back pocket. "Not too busy for you. What can I do to help?"

She blew out an audible breath.

Sideways, he reminded himself. The stress was coming out sideways. If he could put headphones on her and turn up one of her favorite pre-patient-visit 80s girl-band songs, he would. Instead, quietly, he asked, "What's got you worried?"

"If all three mommas deliver, we won't have enough diapers."

Interesting that she wasn't concerned about how she would pull off three deliveries at the same time, which would be his main concern. No, she was only worried that the babies wouldn't have what they needed.

He planted his feet wide and crossed his arms, ready for whatever tension she threw his way. "We'll use kitchen towels like the olden days. What else?"

"What do you mean 'what else'?"

"Come on. Unload on me." He gently tapped her temple. "I know there's more going on up there. Let's hear it."

"Our D-battery supply is low."

"What runs on D batteries?"

"That's not the issue. What if we run out of D batteries?"

"If we need more, we'll pull the batteries from the toy stash in the living room."

She touched her cheek and glanced around the room, as if calculating what she could see, but coming up short. "I was so focused on supplies for the deliveries and babies, I didn't even think about things for the adults."

"All of the basics regarding sleeping arrangements are taken care of. The kitchen is also stocked with everything we'll need if we lose power or water. Paper plates, plastic-ware, disposable cups, and napkins are all ready to go."

"And if the power does go out?"

He nodded. "The generator was tested and it's in working order. And there are also enough candles stored in the dining-room buffet that if we got bored, we could melt and turn them into wax sculptures."

The only reaction she had to his joke was to shift and evaluate something else in the room. "I just feel like we're missing something."

"We're not missing anything, Cora." He took her hand in his, walked her to the kitchen counter, and pointed to each item. "We have the NOAA battery-operated weather radio, eight flashlights of all shapes and sizes with fresh batteries, fully charged bottle warmers, and an old-fashioned can opener with a handle because the one in this house is electric."

Her face softened and she leaned into his side. "You brought a can opener?" she whispered.

"To be able to eat the three months of nonperishable items we have in the pantry."

Finally, she smiled. It was small, but it was real. He'd take it.

Then his phone rang again.

He yanked it out of his pocket and let out an exasperated sigh. He'd ignored too many calls. For all he knew, his business was imploding. "I've got to take this."

Her brow furrowed, and she released his hand and stepped back. "Clearly, you're too busy for this right now."

What was she talking about? He'd been with her all day helping in any way he could. He opened his mouth to say as much, but she held up her hand.

"It's fine. I have things to do."

And then turned on her booted foot and left.

Frustrated, he answered the phone. His voice cracked, betraying his unease. "Blackburn."

"Tri—" The word cut out.

Only one signal bar showed at the top of his screen, but he saw the call had come from his breeder. He walked to the bank of windows in the corner of the living room to see if his phone could get better reception there.

"Clyde? You there?"

"I'm here. The question is, where are you?"

He looked out over the covered porch to the fields beyond. Snow was making a quick cover of the grounds.

"I'm still in Wyoming."

"Whoa. You've got quite the storm coming your way."

Tell me about it.

"I hate to bother you when you're out of town," Clyde continued, "but I don't know what to do. The Jensons received a tough diagnosis for Cara's mother and are leaving town to head to Denver to care for her. Indefinitely. They'll have no acreage at her mother's house to take on your German shepherds like they'd planned."

Tripp grabbed the back of his neck and looked to his boots. The Harletons already had their hands full fostering older puppies that would be ready to train next month. They'd made it clear over the years they didn't like over-lapping litters. Janice Brown declared she needed a break after her last foster experience and requested no new pups until the summer.

"No one's free on my roster of foster families," Tripp said, his mind checking names on his mental list. Typically, he had three to five families in rotation. Now, no one was available? This hadn't happened to him since he'd started his business.

"How long does Maisie have before she delivers?" Tripp asked. He'd already put down a deposit on two of the golden retriever's pups.

"Any day now. But she's not the one I'm worried about."

Tripp knew what was coming, but he didn't know how to solve the problem.

"I can keep Maisie's pups with her while they nurse until you can get here," Clyde said. "But you've got four German shepherds that are weaned and ready to learn the basics. I don't have that kind of time on my hands. And there's one more thing."

Tripp closed his eyes to embrace for impact.

"Melissa called. She still has three weeks left with Bent-ley, but the family coming up to get him need another week and Melissa is going out of town."

His stomach clenched. It was another perfect storm. Pups in various states of training and attention and no-where to put them other than Tripp's land, only Tripp wasn't there to oversee things.

He opened his eyes. "I've got to get home."

"I'm sorry, Tripp. If I could take all of them on for you, I would."

"I know you would, Clyde. I'll head back home." The

skies were grayer than when the call began. "Let me see if I can get out of here before the storm locks me in. It's not looking good, but I'll see what I can do."

Tripp ended the call and blew out a long breath. He had to take care of his business. He could lose clients over this.

But what about his promise to Cora? And he finally felt like he'd been making headway with Haley. He didn't want to leave either of them. But he didn't want to lose business, either.

Rain sidled up to him and knocked Tripp's hand with her nose, then whined. That wasn't a signal for anything Tripp had trained her for.

"What's going on, girl?" he murmured. That wasn't her alert for him to check his heart rate. Definitely not with the added whine. Anyway, he felt fine other than the impending doom to his business. Maybe the storm pressure was throwing her off, he thought as she walked away.

"What's going on?" someone snapped behind him.

He turned and found Haley, arms crossed, her face full of fury with a firm set in her jaw.

"Haley? What's wrong?"

"*What's wrong* is I heard your call. You're leaving. Just like you always do."

His stomach dropped to the floor just as she turned on her heel and stormed away from him.

Cora stood in the office and assessed the items Tripp and Hunter had moved in the room for Karen. They were right to help Karen be as comfortable as possible, especially if she was going to give birth to her baby under uncertain circumstances.

She took in a deep breath, then exhaled slowly, trying to release some of the stress.

Tripp was doing everything in his power to smooth the path for what was coming.

His phone kept ringing. At first, it annoyed her, but she realized she needed to cut him some slack. He had put his entire life on hold to be here. He had a business back home with clients. Just like she did here.

During their picnic, it felt like maybe there was hope for the two of them. *We might be starting to make sense.*

He was kind. Funny. Handsome. And he usually had a keen sense of how to help her in ways that didn't make her feel small. They just made her feel seen.

Her eye caught on a stack of disheveled towels in the corner. She walked over, shaking her head once again over her uneven gait. This ridiculous boot. The good news was at least she wasn't going to deliver a baby on crutches. She picked up the top towel to fold. Holding the end of the towel, she shook it fully open.

Rain walked through the open door.

"Well, hello there," Cora said with a cautious eye on the dog. She'd come to trust Rain over the last few weeks, something she never taught was possible. When she'd pet her at the park, it almost felt normal. But she still wasn't completely comfortable in her presence. "Does Tripp know where you are?"

Rain growled.

Tingles spread from the top of Cora's head down to her toes. Then she realized Tripp must not know where Rain was, otherwise he'd be with her. He told her this morning he would be careful about Rain's whereabouts in the lodge.

But with so many people going in and out of the house with different jobs to prepare for the storm, it wasn't surprising that Tripp had lost track of her.

Still. The growl was new. Not once had Cora heard Rain growl.

Maybe she shouldn't have spoken to the dog.

Or maybe she was just being paranoid.

She finished folding the first towel and picked up the second. She held the ends of the towel and popped this one open.

Rain barked.

Cora's heart pounded.

Rain whined. Growled. Whined.

Whined? Was something wrong?

The Lab licked her paw. Was that blood on her paw?

Cora tucked a towel under one of her arms and leaned down. "What's the matter, girl?"

Rain snapped at her face, then barked. Cora reared back, her chest rising and falling with her breaths.

Did no one in the house hear the bark? She exhaled a long, slow breath. Even if they had, to most people a dog who barked once would seem normal. Most didn't know about Cora's debilitating fear.

But Tripp would have known. Tripp would have come looking.

Rain's growl became louder, and the dog grabbed on to the end of the towel Cora was holding and yanked hard.

Cora screamed and released the towel. She backed farther into the corner. Between her racing heart and quick breaths, she thought she might pass out. She tried to think medically about how to handle her own hyperventilating, but all she could feel was debilitating, unrelenting fear.

Rain growled. Whined. Growled. Whined. She dropped the towel, then lifted a paw.

All Cora could see were sharp toenails. All she could picture was a claw.

Haley appeared in the door and stopped short.

"Get." Cora sucked in a breath. "Tripp."

The girl's eyes went wide. She took a step back, turned her head toward the back of the house, and yelled, "Tripp! Someone get Tripp!"

Cora could hear the pounding of boots coming toward the office, but couldn't take her eyes off Rain. She wanted the walls of her corner to absorb her body into their protection.

Tripp rounded the door and came to a halt alert and quickly assessing. "Rain," he said calmly, but firmly.

His dog turned to him. One growl. One whine. One small lift of a paw.

Cora quietly exhaled. At least the dog wasn't directing her attention to Cora anymore.

He pulled something out of his pocket, crouched down, and held out his hand.

Only Rain scooted back into Cora and bumped into her. And bared her teeth to Tripp.

"Tripp?" Cora said on a strangled breath.

Tripp's next movements were so quick, if she had blinked, she would have missed them. But they were also somehow light and gentle. He slid onto his stomach, placing his body closer to his dog's, and dropped a treat in front of her. Distracted by the treat, Rain dipped her head lower just enough for Tripp to push up, come across the top of her head with one hand to grab her snout shut, and pull the dog's body down parallel with his while securing her to his side.

He murmured words to Rain that Cora couldn't make out.

All Cora could do was stare.

"Walk out of the room, Cora," he said to her with a tight voice. "Don't run, just walk."

Only she was frozen. She heard his words. She knew it was safe to leave.

"Cora, sweetheart, it's okay." Tripp turned into Rain farther, shielding her even more from the dog. "All you're going to do is take one step at a time past me. Past *me*. Walk right past my back and into the hallway."

Suddenly, Haley was there, grasping Cora's hand in hers, and leading her out of the room.

Cora wasn't sure how long she sat on the living-room couch, or who had placed a hot cup of tea in her hands, or when exactly the tears started running down her cheeks.

She only knew staring into the fire was comforting, so that's where her focus stayed until she felt someone sit next to her on the couch.

Slowly, she looked into a set of very beautiful, very concerned blue eyes.

"Hey," Tripp whispered.

"Hey," she whispered back.

His eyes roamed over her face and stopped at her cheeks. He lifted a hand, placing his palm on her cheek, and thumbed away the tear streaks.

"What I'm going to say," he said, his voice thick, "isn't going to make everything right. But I'd like to explain Rain's actions, if that's okay."

This man. This man who was always giving her a choice.

She nodded.

"She was hurt," he said, something fierce working behind his eyes.

"Hurt?"

"I'm not saying what happened was okay. She broke her orders in regard to you." He took her hand in his and squeezed. "But I don't think she was going to harm you, Cora. I think she needed help."

Cora thought about the growl and the whine. It was almost like Rain was conflicted, moving back and forth between emotions. Cora could relate.

Fresh, hot tears hit her cheeks. "Is she okay?" she whispered.

"She's fine." There was relief in Tripp's voice. But something battled in his eyes. "This was my fault."

"Why would you think that?"

"Everything's been so crazy." He let out a breath and stared at the floor. "I should have… She came to me." He looked up at her, agony in his face. "She came to me and gave me a confusing signal. Not anything that we'd worked on. I should have stopped what I was doing and checked on her."

His phone. He was distracted by his phone.

"With the fresh snow covering the ground, she stepped in a pile of something not good and ended up with three splinters in one of her paws. Two small ones and one big sliver. Dogs can be sensitive about their feet, and injuries make everything harder."

She drew her fingertips to her mouth and whispered, "She was licking her paw."

"I think so," he whispered back. "And I'm just so sorry, Cora."

She pulled her hand down from her mouth and placed it on his arm. "Where is she?"

"I put her in her kennel. But not before I walked her to the doorway of the living room and reestablished my command to not approach you."

"Where's her kennel?"

"It's in the dining room for now. I didn't want her to have to walk up the stairs on her hurt paw to her room. I hope that's okay."

"It's fine. But—" How was she going to fix this? "Would it be confusing to her if I went and talked to her through the kennel door? Or if I…" She huffed out a breath. Was she ready to do it? "If I pet her through the door?"

He considered her. "I'm not sure. It's important to re-establish commands and positive feedback for obedience. I don't want to confuse her. Especially after what happened."

Cora felt confused. Maybe she and Rain could bond over their joint confusion with the man in front of her.

"Cora," Tripp said. "I'm just so very sorry."

A short, almost curt-sounding sigh came from behind the couch. "Oh, did he tell you?"

She looked back and saw Haley standing with her arms crossed over her chest, accenting her small baby bump.

"Tell me what?" Cora asked.

"Haley," Tripp said quickly in a rebuking tone.

What had happened between these two that Cora didn't know about?

"He's leaving," his half sister said, causing Cora's world to spin.

She looked to Tripp. "You're leaving?" she asked, her voice sounding like sandpaper while hurt moved through her veins.

"I—" Tripp ran a hand down his face, then looked at his sister as if torn. "I'm sorry, Hay-Bear."

Haley propped her arms up farther on her chest and glared at her half brother while a lone tear streaked down her cheek.

He focused on Cora. "A foster family had to back out,

and for various reasons, the others aren't available. I have four German shepherds who are about to be without a home. And another who is going to need a home soon. Much less the puppies that are due any day now that the breeder is taking on out of the kindness of his heart."

That sounded like a lot. She tried. She tried so hard to let empathy override her hurting heart. But at the bottom of it all, he was going to leave.

"My business and reputation are on the line," he said in a thick voice.

She couldn't ask him to stay. Couldn't ask him to choose her over his business in Colorado. That wouldn't be fair to him, the same way it wouldn't be fair for him to ask her to drop all her pregnant clients and leave Wyoming.

So they weren't starting to make sense. They weren't starting to make sense at all.

"I'm sorry, Cora," he said in a low voice and sounded truly regretful. "I need to get back as soon as possible. I can't run my business from here right now."

"Well, you're not going anywhere anytime soon," Hunter said, leaning against the doorframe, arms crossed and a displeased look on his face.

When had he shown up?

Her brother glanced at her and softened his voice. "You okay?"

Ah. Protective-brother mode. Someone must have gone for him after the incident with Rain.

"Yeah," she said. When he raised his eyebrows in doubt, she added, "I'm fine. Promise."

"Why isn't Tripp going anywhere anytime soon?" Haley asked, the reminder like a ton of bricks hitting Cora's stomach. Tripp wanted to leave.

Hunter nodded his chin in the direction of the window. "The pass is blocked."

Tripp stood, intensity coming off him as he walked to the tall windows and stared outside.

With the impending snowstorm, it seemed it wasn't just the expecting mommas feeling ill at ease. The entire house seemed on edge.

Certainly, her heart felt that way.

Chapter Ten

The storm hit more quickly than anyone anticipated. Over the course of the night, the massive blizzard made it abundantly clear that Tripp, Rain, and Haley would also be staying at the lodge for the duration.

After pacing a patch of hardwood flooring in front of the windows for hours, Tripp finally fell asleep on a leather recliner in the living room, arms crossed, mind reeling over his situation.

He awoke to the heavily booted steps of Dalton looking for Cora. When he glanced at his watch, it was 4:00 a.m.

He pushed down the footrest on the recliner and sat up. While working a crick out of his neck, he listened to Dalton tell Cora that Karen had been in active labor all night and was nearing transition, whatever that meant. Tripp didn't have all the terminology down.

That's when he saw Cora's expression go into full warrior-midwife mode.

"Tell her I'll be right there." She went to the kitchen sink and used a special soap to wash her hands and lower arms.

Tripp rubbed his eyes and walked over to her.

"She'll deliver fast," she said. "It's her fourth, and her other deliveries went well."

He pulled his earbuds out of his pocket, placed them in

her ears, and pressed Play on her going-to-work playlist, the volume set low, so she could still hear conversation.

She nodded once, still laser-focused on her hands.

After pulling a spoon out of one of the kitchen drawers, he turned and leaned his hips against the counter space next to her. His other pocket held a package of Skittles. Once he opened them, he scooped some out with the spoon and held them close to her mouth.

She blanched, looking first at the spoon, then at him.

"Open up," he said softly. "My girl needs her pregame ritual."

A flash of affection crossed her face, then disappeared once she accepted his offering and got back to scrubbing her fingernails.

Maybe she had forgiven him. Maybe not. But now wasn't the time to have that discussion. And it felt like there was so much to talk about. He didn't want to leave her. And if he didn't leave, he wanted to be able to tell her that they had a future. Maybe. If she felt the same way.

He just couldn't solve everything with his business right now. He didn't know what kind of a timeline he had.

Did she even feel the same way? Would she want him to move his business here and settle so soon in a relationship?

Maybe he should back up a moment. Did she like him at all?

A flush-faced Chase strode into the room, a purposeful look on his face. He locked eyes with his sister. "Lexi's having contractions."

If Tripp hadn't watched Cora in action the last few weeks, he might have missed the almost imperceptible tightness around her eyes.

But she smiled at her brother. "That's good news, Chase. This is her first baby, so we may have a while—"

"They're two to three minutes apart."

Again, Tripp saw the stress. Only this time, it was bracketed around her lips.

And again, only calm and confidence came from her. "Wonderful. We've got this, Chase. I'm going to check on Karen and then I'll head to Lexi. Is she still in the guest bedroom?"

Chase paled. "Karen's in labor, too?"

"Yes. Don't worry. We got this, Chase."

He coursed a hand through his hair. "C-can you do that? Deliver two babies at the same time?"

"Chase." Cora's tone changed to a directive. "I am not your little sister right now. I'm your midwife. I know you had a doctor lined up to do this job, but I'm good at what I do. I need you to trust me. Can you do that?"

Chase looked around the room, then took a deep breath. When he looked back to Cora, he nodded once. "I can do that."

"We've got this," she repeated, offering a small smile. "Now, go be with your strong, beautiful wife. She needs you by her side. I'll be there in a minute."

The second Chase left the room, Cora turned off the water with her elbow, looked down into the sink, and let out a long breath.

Tripp turned to her and stepped forward. "You've got this," he said while removing the earbuds.

She turned her head and leaned her forehead into his chest.

Maybe she did like Tripp.

Or maybe he just needed to keep his head in the game, because things were about to get busy around here. Really busy.

"Two babies at the same time," she whispered so softly he could barely hear her.

He wrapped an arm around her shoulders. "What can I do?"

With one final breath in and out, she pulled away from him and he let his arm drop. She shook off whatever moment she was having, and said, "Can you please find Haley and send her to check on Lexi? I think she fell asleep on the couch."

"Absolutely."

After rousing Haley, Tripp positioned himself in the hallway halfway between the office and the guest room, leaning against the wall, arms crossed, head down. Tripp wasn't sure what went on behind those closed doors, but every time someone exited one of the rooms, he looked in that direction and waited to see if anyone needed something.

He found himself fetching glasses of water, ice, and switching out towels and washrags for clean ones. It was about all he was good for. Once, he tried to stop Cora to get her to drink something, but she outright snapped at him.

Then she apologized. And returned to calmly, but fiercely, take care of the labors of two women. At the same time. All while handling their husbands, one of whom was her brother, as if she was herding cattle and in total control. She was as impressive as she was dazzling. He couldn't take his eyes off her when she passed him.

On the other hand, Tripp felt useless. Hanging his head low, he rubbed the back of his neck.

The smell of coffee wafted through the hallway. He didn't know how long he'd been standing there. Long enough to know that both women were going to have their babies pretty close together. Long enough to know Cora was handling each birth calmly and proficiently.

Yeah, he was useless. She didn't need him today. Maybe she didn't need him in her life at all.

Something ached in his chest. He rubbed at the spot.

Hunter entered the foyer and handed him a cup of coffee. He leaned up against the wall, too, and waited.

"You'll have a niece or a nephew pretty soon."

Pride radiated from the soon-to-be uncle. "Yeah," he said. "But hopefully he or she will take after Lexi. Anything's better than Chase's ugly mug."

Amused, Tripp tapped his coffee to Hunter's in agreement.

Suddenly they heard a newborn baby's cry from the office.

Dalton rushed out of the room and declared, "It's a girl!"

"That's great," said Tripp.

"Congratulations," called Hunter.

The new father turned on his heel and headed back to his wife and new baby girl.

Chase marched out of the guest bedroom and the men turned to look at him. "Cora?" Chase called, his teeth clenched tight.

In what must have felt like years to Chase, but in reality was only about thirty seconds, Cora stepped out of the office drying her hands off with a towel.

"Lexi says she thinks it's time," he said, stress laced in each word.

Cora nodded. "Then let's go," she said nonchalantly, as if she was headed down to the store to check on the price of eggs. She shoved the towel into Tripp's hands as she passed by, never looking at him.

Totally in the zone. She was something else.

The spot on his chest zinged, and he rubbed it with his fingers.

"Stop drooling over my sister, dude," Hunter said, pulling Tripp out of his thoughts. "Also, your dog's whining."

He didn't know which to address first. It was probably best to ignore the sister comment.

Rain. He'd let her out once this morning to feed her, but promptly put her back in the kennel. After what happened yesterday, he didn't want anything distracting Cora. Especially now. But he felt badly for his dog.

"She shouldn't need to go out again so soon," Tripp murmured. He felt torn between supporting the woman he was beginning to hold close to his heart and the dog who was his closest companion.

He'd wait a few more minutes.

Both men stared at their boots and, every so often, took sips of their coffee.

A squeak or a coo would come from the office. Muffled words of encouragement would come from the guest bedroom.

Soon, another newborn cry sounded, this time from Lexi's room.

Hunter turned to Tripp, a smile wide on his face.

"Congratulations, man." Tripp pulled Hunter in and pounded him on the back with a congratulatory hug.

The door opened, and Chase emerged holding a precious pink-faced baby. His wide smile matched his twin's, but his held a little more relief. And pride. "I'd like to introduce you all to Noelle Cross."

Surprise crossed Hunter's face, followed but something peaceful. "After Mom," he said, his voice thick.

Chase nodded.

"How's Lexi doing?" Tripp asked.

Chase bounced the baby gently, looking like a pro, not like a first-time father.

Cora stepped out of the room, a soft glow of satisfaction on her face.

She was the most beautiful thing Tripp had ever seen.

"Lexi was a superhero through the whole thing," Chase said.

But Tripp could only look at Cora. Formidable. Unshakable. Almost unfathomable. So much talent in that small body of hers.

Haley came out of Karen's room and closed the door gently.

"Everything go okay?" Cora asked.

"Yes. Baby is feeding well now. They're all resting."

Cora squeezed Haley's arm. "You up for checking on Lexi?"

"Sure thing." Haley stepped into the guest bedroom.

Tripp could feel his mouth gaping. Apparently, his little sister was more capable than he thought. If she could stay so calm during two births and help the mommas afterward, he had the feeling she and her baby were going to be just fine.

She wouldn't need him, either.

Cora cooed at the baby. Totally mesmerized by the tiny person in her brother's arms. Her niece. Her mother's namesake.

Rain whined from the dining room. Tripp felt like he was intruding on a family moment, and excused himself to check on his dog.

When he hit the dining room, Cora was on his heels. "Where are you going?"

He glanced to the kennel and turned to her. "I need to

let Rain out. And I've got to figure out when we can get out of here."

Hurt slashed across her face. "So that's it? You're really just going to leave?"

"Cora, you don't need me."

"What do you mean?"

"You handled today like it was any other day of the week. Like delivering two babies in a snowstorm is normal." She started to say something, but he shook his head. Frustration bubbled in him, and he struggled to figure out how to explain it to her. "It's the way you do life. You just handle everything on your own. I don't know if it's that you don't trust me, or you don't trust anyone, or maybe you don't need to trust anyone because you can handle things in your life on your own."

She looked like he had slapped her. She whispered, "Where is this coming from?"

Oh, man. He was totally messing this up. He wanted to tell her how he felt about her. Instead, he'd done the opposite.

"Is this how *you* do life, Tripp? You swoop in and fix everything you can, decide you aren't needed anymore, and then take off?"

Whoa. He stood speechless in front of her.

She turned to leave and got as far as the door before she angled her body back toward him. "Why do you care, anyway, Tripp? You're leaving. Right?"

"Cora," he pleaded.

Rain whined behind him.

Then Tripp shook his head. She was right. He was leaving. He released a long sigh of resignation. "Yeah. I have to go."

"Right," she said curtly. "Then just go." She walked out the door, taking a piece of his heart with her.

Hours later, babies and new mommas settled, pregnant mommas checked on, Cora put the earbuds Tripp had left her into her ears. He'd texted her that she'd find them tucked on a shelf in the pantry, sent her a link to a playlist with her "After" songs, and let her know she would find privacy in the pantry if she needed a few minutes to herself.

Thoughtful, kind, and frustrating man.

She slid down the wall of the pantry, tucked her legs into her body, and wrapped her arms around her knees. She hit Play on the list and rested her head on her knees.

Curled in a cocoon, hidden away, for just a few moments, Cora let loose every emotion she was holding on to in her head. In her heart.

Tears streamed down her cheeks. Her chest convulsed with the release. She gasped.

She'd been up all night checking on all the details in the house, and had only taken a catnap. The next thing she knew, she was running back and forth between two deliveries. Handling each expectant momma and husband with care. Dealing with the delivery of an experienced mom. And the delivery of a new mom, one who had been on bed rest, her sister-in-law.

She'd simply absorbed all the stress and tried to do her best to deal with it. One step at a time.

In the end, she'd managed two healthy deliveries. The other two mothers tucked in the snowed-in house had no contractions.

Then why did this release feel worse than others?

Because she had needed Tripp's help.

"He was amazing," she whispered to herself. He'd anticipated her needs. He'd stood by her, been solid, supportive, and calm. She could feel his unwavering belief in her.

Even now, she sat hidden, able to release the tension of the day, because he knew she would need to. He'd even swept the pantry for her because he knew she would need a private place.

What was wrong with her that she couldn't put her trust in him?

She rubbed her forehead back and forth against her knees.

"What is wrong with me?" she whispered, wiping the tears from her face.

When she got up, she peeked out the pantry door. When the coast was clear, she grabbed a trash bag and headed to empty the trashcans around the house. But something on the back porch caught her eye.

Rain.

Pacing back and forth, whimpering.

Was she okay?

Cora looked around, but no one was to be found. Both newborns were tucked away with their families, and she wasn't about to ask for help from the new parents. Where was Hunter? She texted him in case he was close by.

After grabbing her coat, she carefully, on full alert, inched the back door open and stepped onto the back porch.

Rain whimpered. Whined. Looked across the land, back to her. Whined again. She paced back and forth. Whined. Looked to the acreage beyond, then back to her. Whined.

What in the world?

Cora's head was so tempted to fall into panic, but her heart wanted her to stay present. Listen to the dog.

A dog that looked like she was trying to tell Cora something, but knew she shouldn't approach.

Could that be it? Rain knows she shouldn't approach Cora, but something was wrong? "I don't want to confuse you," Cora said in a low voice, getting on her haunches and holding out her hand. "But I think you're trying to talk to me. And Tripp said that I have to make the first move."

At the sound of Tripp's name, Rain practically jumped out of her skin. She turned to the field and flat-out barked. Once. Then turned to look at Cora as if that should mean something.

"Is it Tripp?"

Rain repeated her actions, this time a little more frantically. Which seeped into Cora's bones.

It had to be Tripp.

Cora shot off a text to Hunter that she thought something was wrong with Tripp and was heading out with Rain. She pulled a trash bag over her booted foot and secured it tightly. It would make for awkward walking, but hopefully keep the snow at bay. She pulled her gloves out of her pocket and tugged them on her hands, then yanked her snowcap over her head.

"Let's go, Rain. Find Tripp." She had no idea if that was even a command for the dog, but Rain seemed to understand.

Cora tamped down the rising panic and concentrated on keeping her footing in the snow. Maybe if she was taller than five foot two, she wouldn't feel like the snow was trying to swallow her whole. It didn't matter. Soon she wouldn't feel anything because the freezing temperature was settling in .

"Tripp!" she called out. A few steps later, she yelled his name again.

Rain didn't stop to acknowledge her yelling. She would only run toward the backside of the property, run back to Cora, then when she was within five feet of her, turn back and run toward the same place again.

As they approached the tree line, a howl in the distance called out. A wretched cold seeped down Cora's spine that had nothing to do with the snow. Instead, it felt eerie.

Cora paused, fear infiltrating her focus to find Tripp.

Rain whined at Lexi, turned to the trees, and barked.

Something that looked unnatural caught her eye about ten yards ahead in the forest. Colors that didn't make sense. A piece of clothing. Tripp's Carhartt jacket?

Cora tried to move more quickly through the snow. She fell once on the hard ground of the forest, feeling the strain in her ankle, then got up to push forward. She practically slid to his side when she reached him.

Tripp. On the ground. Unmoving, his right hand over his heart.

"Tripp!" She felt for a pulse and found one. But it was too fast. He was breathing, but he needed help. Bacterial endocarditis. That's what he had said. That he might need a valve replacement someday. Had Rain missed the symptoms? Or had Tripp ignored the alerts?

Cora had no idea because she had been so wrapped up in her own world.

She framed his face in her hands. "Tripp? Tripp, I need you to wake up, baby. I need you to wake up. Can you hear me? It's Cora."

In the distance, the howl sounded off again, this time with an answering howl. There were two now. Were they closer than last time?

Rain stood on alert, the hairs at her neck standing

straight up. She growled in the direction of the howls, then looked back at Tripp.

Cora needed help. And the one person who told her she was bad at asking for help was the very reason she needed help. What did he say earlier? That she didn't trust him.

No, that wasn't it. Or it wasn't it entirely.

She didn't trust God.

She didn't know if God was with her when she was seventeen. She wanted to believe He was.

I will never leave you, nor forsake you. That's what God said in the Bible.

The howls came closer, then they switched to barking. She could hear the wolves running. How many, she didn't know. They usually came in packs, but it didn't sound like a large one.

Her heart pounded. Her leg throbbed. She squeezed her eyes closed. "Lord. Help."

It was all she could muster.

Rain growled something ferocious. She even looked bigger, like she had puffed out her chest and was straining to be tall.

"Tripp?" She placed her cheek next to his and spoke in his ear. "Tripp, please. We have to go. Wake up. We have to go."

Something sounded behind her. She turned and strained her eyes to see. Was that a snowmobile?

Yes!

The sounds of the wolves and the snowmobile both increased in volume. They were both headed straight for her, the wolves from the forest, the snowmobile from the ranch. Rain's body strung taut with tension, her focus on the forest danger.

Cora bent over Tripp and shielded his face. "Tripp, Tripp, Tripp," she whispered.

The snowmobile finally reached them, sliding sideways to a stop, spraying snow into the trees. "Cora?"

Hunter. She didn't dare move. Just as she was about to call his name, a shotgun fired.

Cora's breaths turned rapid. *Don't panic, don't panic, don't panic.*

The barking changed direction, the sounds becoming more distant.

She heard the crunching of steps coming toward her, felt a hand on her shoulder, heard her brother's voice. "Cora, they're gone. They're gone," Hunter said.

Cora looked into her brother's hazel stare. "They're g-gone?"

"They're gone. You're safe." He looked down. "What's going on here?"

They're gone. She was safe. She inhaled through her nose and let the oxygen calm her. She wiggled her toes in her shoes to ground her to the moment.

Tripp.

"He has a heart issue. Rain alerts him to the symptoms, but I think in all the confusion of the day, he missed what Rain was telling him. His heart rate's too rapid to be safe. We need to get him to a hospital. Now."

Chapter Eleven

Tripp didn't know how he got to the hospital, but whoever had gotten him there probably saved his life.

He studied the screen monitoring his heart activity. Everything looked normal now, but he knew that wasn't the case yesterday. He was grateful that Dr. Flavan had been snowed in at the hospital. The cardiologist usually rotated through the smaller hospitals in the area and wasn't scheduled to be anywhere near Elk Run yesterday. But he'd been at the hospital and was able to pull Tripp's heart out of A-Fib quickly. Only to deliver the news that it was indeed time for Tripp's valve to be replaced.

How could he have ignored Rain's warnings? His doctors told him at every visit that someday the damage from the bacterial endocarditis would finally require the valve replacement. Tripp knew better than to dismiss Rain's actions. He'd trained other people to be more attuned to their canine alerts than that. Trained his dog to know better on Tripp's behalf so he would be safe.

The error was his and his alone.

He slid a hand through his hair, accidentally pulling on the IV tube he'd forgotten about. "Ouch," he murmured.

"Everything okay?" a deep voice boomed from the doorway.

"Other than the drafty hospital gown I'm wearing and this IV, just dandy." Tripp looked up as he was untangling the IV tube from an EKG cord. "Come on in, Hunter."

Hunter ambled to a chair beside Tripp's hospital bed and sat down, stretching his jean-clad legs out in front of him and holding a disposable coffee cup between his hands. He said nothing and everything all at the same time. Tripp recalled a deployment where Chase explained this phenomenon to him, but he'd never believed the hype. Now, he knew the truth. Chase hadn't exaggerated.

Tripp's throat clogged, and he cleared it. "You saved my life, didn't you?"

Hunter shook his head. "Rain did that. And Cora."

"Cora?" But how could that be? Rain would have had to get someone for help. That's what she was trained to do. "That's not possible. She's terrified of dogs. Rain wouldn't have gone to her."

Hunter only stared at him blankly.

"She did, didn't she?" Tripp sighed and scratched at the stubble that had grown on his cheek, pulling at the IV again. He couldn't help himself when he let out a small growl at the tubing. He knew better. He'd put Cora in a terrible position if Rain had gone to her.

Tripp had taken his stupid walk to work out some of his frustrations. He'd been so angry. Maybe felt a little misunderstood, too. He couldn't help Cora. Couldn't make her understand. Certainly not under the stress of the impending births. But he'd most definitely failed her when Rain had sought her out. She must have been terrified. But he couldn't fault his dog. Rain was trained to be quite verbal and convincing if she knew Tripp needed help.

"He took care of her," Hunter murmured into his coffee cup just before he took a drink.

"He? Who is he?"

"God."

Tripp cocked his head. "God took care of her?"

"The wolves were close."

Panic skittered through Tripp's spine. "No," he whispered.

"God took care of her when she was seventeen," Hunter said, pain flashing in his eyes, "and He took care of her yesterday."

"Is she okay?"

The man took another swig of his coffee. "I already told you."

"Right. God took care of her," Tripp said, then closed his eyes and shook his head. God took care of Cora yesterday.

"I know you know Chase better than you know me. Known him longer. But you and I are cut from the same cloth."

Tripp opened his eyes and focused on Hunter. A few weeks ago, he'd been a stranger. Now, he was somehow an ally. "What cloth is that?"

"The one that thinks they're responsible for everyone else."

"We aren't cut from the same cloth, Hunter. You quit everything to raise your siblings. I abandoned my little sister when she needed me most."

"And what happened to her?"

Then it hit Tripp square in the chest. God took care of Haley. Tripp had no clue how to care for his sister. He'd left his sister high and dry. His throat clogged with emotion. "God led her to Wyoming and straight back to Him."

"Yup." Hunter nodded. "Trust."

"What?"

"Trust. I told this to Chase when he was struggling, and I'll tell you the same. That's the choice we get. To trust God with the things that were His to begin with."

"But she's my sister."

"And Cora's mine. But you'll still have to trust God with her." Slowly, Hunter nodded.

Was he giving them his approval? Certainly his advice, which might be an indirect way to show his approval.

Then another realization hit Tripp. He was a hypocrite.

His entire argument with Cora had been about trusting God, and apparently he couldn't seem to do it himself.

But maybe God didn't need Tripp to handle everything. Maybe Tripp just needed to trust.

"I'd like to make you an offer," Hunter said, standing up to throw away his coffee cup.

"Whatever it is, I hope I can do it from Colorado. I've got to get back."

"You're not going to be able to run that business the way you want to for a while."

"What do you mean?"

"You've got a surgery coming up, don't you?"

"How did you know?" Tripp closed his eyes. "Cora. Cora knows what yesterday meant." He blew out a long breath. "Yes. I have a valve-replacement surgery that needs to get done. The sooner, the better."

"Chase and I would like for you to bring your business here. You can use our acreage for your business, but eventually we'd like you to head up the dog-therapy program we want to house at Four Cross as part of the nonprofit."

It was a good offer. One he should consider. But Tripp shook his head. "That's very nice of you guys. But as much as I'd like to be here, the bulk of my business is in Colorado. All my contacts, my foster families, my vet."

He looked out the window to the mountains beyond. With his relationship with his half sister on the rocks, and his relationship with Cora ending before it even had a chance to begin, Tripp needed to decline the offer.

"I appreciate the offer. I really do." He heard a nurse enter the room but didn't greet her. "But I've got to get back home."

"So that's how it's going to be?"

He turned back from the window to see Cora standing at the foot of his bed.

So it hadn't been a nurse that entered his room.

It was a stormy woman, with her arms crossed, fierce eyes, and…was that his dog at her feet?

It felt like Tripp was abandoning her.

But she knew that wasn't fair to him.

She felt like she was in a tug-of-war with herself, desperately wanting to keep Tripp in Wyoming and letting him go in the same breath so she didn't get hurt.

She'd almost lost Tripp. Maybe it was better for him to leave Elk Run in one piece.

But then she'd miss him.

Her emotions were all over the map right now. And the truth was, she was just so glad he was alright. She tried humor instead, but even as the words came out of her mouth, she could tell they fell flat. "I braved my first helicopter trip with you on board, and this is how you thank me? By leaving?"

Questions flew across Tripp's face. "How did a helicopter get to me?"

Hunter jumped in to explain. "The snow blew out as fast as it came in."

Rain started whining, her tail swishing the ground at an almost alarming rate.

Tripp held out his hand. "Come."

The dog didn't have to be told twice. She galloped to her owner's bed and was up on hind legs, straining her head to kiss him. Now, her tail wagged ferociously and threatened to smack anything within its radius.

"I know, I know," Tripp said, allowing the onslaught of affection from Rain. "Calm, girl," he murmured, then tucked his head in her shoulder.

Cora felt like she was intruding and stepped back.

"You tried to tell me," Tripp said into the dog's wiggling coat. "You tried to tell me."

Hunter turned to walk out of the room but stopped by Cora's side. He put his hand on her shoulder and offered a tender squeeze. A sweet display of brotherly affection that he gave no one but her. "He likes you, you know. Don't be an idiot."

So much for brotherly affection. "Why would you—"

"You both look at each other the same way."

She should have known Hunter would be perceptive. When he became her guardian, she never got away with anything. It was no different now.

"It's not that simple," she whispered.

"It is."

"I can't wait until someone steals your heart, Hunter Cross," she said under her breath. "It's going to be so fun to watch you fall in love."

He gave her another squeeze and left the room.

She should probably have left, too. But her heart wouldn't let her. Tripp was fine. But she needed another moment to see it for herself.

Tripp had gripped both sides of Rain's face and nuzzled his dog. He finally pulled back and looked at Cora. "Thank you." His voice sounded deep. Thick. Full of so much more than two simple words.

Tears hit the back of her eyes, but she wouldn't let them fall. "You're welcome," she whispered.

Rain pushed off the bed, came to Cora's side, then turned and sat at attention next to her.

The side of Tripp's mouth twitched. "Are you trying to steal my dog?"

"She won't leave my side."

Concern hit his eyes. "Is that okay with you?"

"A lot has happened since you decided to take a nap in the woods. I've become quite a dog lover." She offered him a small smile. "At least this dog."

"Why don't you sit down—" he nodded to the chair next to his bed "—and fill me in on everything I missed."

When she sat down, he held out his hand. She took a long look at him then took it in hers. She began to relay the events of the day. As if she was filling out a medical chart. When she finished, she said, "I'm so glad you're okay."

He brushed his thumb over the top of her hand. "Do you want to talk about handling Rain when you didn't know what was going on?"

"No."

"The wolves?"

"No."

"How you've been running all over this hospital taking care of your patients and checking on me?"

"I haven't—"

He raised his eyebrows. "Careful. Remember, I know you well."

"No." She sat up straighter. "I don't want to talk about it."

He sighed. "Cora, you're the bravest person I know."

"You say it like it's a bad thing."

"It's not a bad thing," he said, looking at her. "I'm just sorry that not only was I not able to help with any of this, but I was the cause of most of it. I put Rain in the crate and missed all of her signals."

Guilt flooded her. "You put Rain in the crate because of her interaction with me. Because I can't handle dogs. This is *my* fault."

He shook his head. "You can't think that. I had a plan, and it didn't work."

"It did work. Everything happened the way it was supposed to happen. You had everything in place for the moment your heart needed help."

"Except I would never have planned for my bad valve to finally spring a leak and for Rain to run to you."

She looked down at their hands. "I'm glad I was the one she came to find. You would have been so proud of her."

As if she knew they were talking about her, Rain sidled up to Cora and leaned on her leg.

A half smile crossed Tripp's face. One that was part amusement, part concern. "You sure you're okay with her at your side?"

"Rain is nothing but respectful and loving." *Like her owner*, Cora wanted to add. At least, sometimes she thought she felt love from Tripp.

A smile tugged at his lips. "You sure you're not trying to steal my dog?"

Cora shook her head. "Not a chance. You're going to need her."

He nodded.

"You're also going to need help when they replace that valve."

"I know," he said quietly.

"Did the doctor say how soon you need to have it done?"

"Soon."

She swallowed. Here it comes. She'd been thinking about this. Hoping. "You could come here and get it done. I could help you. Drive you where you need to go."

His shoulders shook, and it looked like he was holding back a smile. But failing miserably. "Thank you," he said, and coughed.

She pulled her hand out of his and crossed her arms. "Why do you say it like that?"

He held up his hands in a placating manner. "I think that after a surgery like that, it's important that the patient not be put under any kind of strain."

"My driving causes you strain?"

"Your driving causes the Department of Transportation to rethink the legal age of driving."

The smile that hit her face could not be helped. "Well, I could do other things for you. I could cook."

He cocked his head. "Do you even know how to cook?"

"Point taken. I could get takeout from the diner." She raised her index finger. "And if I ran errands for you, you wouldn't have to be in the car with me. That way, I could do something for you and not put your heart in danger."

He seared a look into her and whispered, "My heart's in danger anytime it's around you."

She whispered back, "I don't want you to leave."

"I don't, either." He took her hand again. "But I could lose my business if I don't get home and take care of things. I need to find new dog foster families as soon as possible so I can get the valve replacement scheduled. If I can't find new families to help, I'll have to stay home to take care of each litter. I'd lose my traveling business. I'm known for hand-delivering the trained puppies to families and working with them in their homes for a few days while they all adjust. If I lose that aspect of my business, my clientele decreases, and I can't make ends meet."

Tripp wasn't abandoning her. He needed to go home for work. And she needed to let him.

If she didn't leave soon, the tears that pricked her eyes were going to fall, and she wasn't sure if she'd be able to walk out the door. She cleared her throat and tried to steady her voice. "When do you head back to Colorado?"

"As soon as they'll let me out of here." He paused, then grimaced. "I'd like to have lunch with Haley before I get on the road, but I'm not sure she's speaking to me."

"You can handle the emotions of a soldier with PTSD. Why can't you handle the emotions of a pregnant woman?"

"Because this woman is my sister, who has every right to be angry at me."

Cora stood. "Maybe she's not angry, Tripp. Maybe she just misses you."

"I miss her, too." He stared at her and said in a low tone, "I'm going to miss you, as well."

"Me, too," she said softly. She ran her knuckles down his arm, smiled what felt like a sad smile, and got up to leave.

Only Rain stepped toward the door with her.

Cora stopped. Rain did the same and sat. Cora kneeled down, Rain looking at her expectantly, and wrapped her arms around the dog's neck. "Thank you," she whispered.

When Cora stood, she motioned to Rain, "Stay with Tripp."

Once the dog returned to her owner's side, Cora said, "I hope your heart heals well," and walked out the door.

Making her way down the hall, a miserable sadness

enveloped her. She wanted to stay with Tripp, too. With each step farther from him, her heart hurt. Her pain might be for different reasons than Tripp's, but hers would most definitely need time to heal as well.

Chapter Twelve

After one more night of observation, Tripp was released from the hospital the next day, and got a text from his sister that almost sounded friendly. He headed to the ranch, cleaned up, threw on some jeans and a Henley, and packed up his things. When he walked into the Elk Run Diner, Rain at his side, the bell jangled over his head.

Stacy approached him with a smile and said excitedly, "Biscuits and gravy, you won't believe what happened! Your sister walked right in here and ordered the Partridge in a Pear Tree. She's waiting for you to start eating."

He grinned at her. "I guess I'd better go help her, then."

Tripp made it to the table and dropped into the booth across from Haley. Rain settled at his feet.

Haley stared at him. The blue ruffly shirt she had on brought out the blue in her eyes, but couldn't erase the look of concern on her face. "Are you okay?"

Her demeanor was so completely the opposite of the hostility she'd thrown at him a few days ago, he shook his head to make sure he was reading her correctly. "Am I okay?"

"Tripp, the last I saw you, you were being whisked away in a helicopter." She curled a lock of hair behind her ear. "I was so worried. I didn't want to come to the hospital because, well, I didn't think you'd want to see me after our argument."

Her words took him aback. "Haley, I will always want to see you."

She swallowed. "So…are you okay?"

He reached across the table and left his palm up for her. She placed her hand in his. "I'm fine. It's time to get that heart valve replaced. My body was just letting me know."

"Well, I don't care for how it let you know."

"I had Rain with me. She got help," he said calmly. Firmly. "And now, I'm fine."

"Fine, except you're going to have heart surgery."

"It's going to be okay, Haley." He squeezed her hand. "They do this surgery all the time."

"I don't know—" She shook her head and when she looked at him, he saw the sheen of moisture in her eyes. "I don't know what I would have done without you. What I'll do if something happens to you."

She swiped a tear from her cheek.

It was time to set things right. Not because Haley was worried about losing him. But because he had decided that he was going to be a solid part of her life moving forward. It was something he should have done a long time ago.

"Hay-Bear." He waited until she looked at him. "I'm so sorry that I wasn't able to care for you when you needed me. Will you forgive me?"

She shook her head, as if not quite understanding. "There's no need for that now. It doesn't matter."

"Yes, it does. Will you forgive me?"

She paused, then whispered, "Yes."

He closed his eyes, felt her forgiveness in his heart, then opened them. "And I want to ask you if it'd be okay if I was part of your life. Part of my nephew's life. I want to help. But also, I just—I just want to know you. You're my family."

She smiled a watery smile at him. "I'd really like that."

"I'll try to visit when I can. Maybe I can carve out time to be here the first week or so of the baby's life to help with all-nighters."

Her smile grew.

"But fair warning," he said, "I have no idea how to change a diaper."

She sat up straight and said proudly, "I'll teach you."

"Yeah," he said, realizing that his little sister was not so little anymore. "I think you have a lot you could teach me. But first—" he nodded to the Partridge in a Pear Tree "—we've got to get started on this thing if we have a chance at beating it."

She scooped up a bite of pancake and then pointed her fork at him. "I should tell you some things about Cora."

A piece of bacon made it halfway to his mouth, then stopped at Cora's name. He raised an eyebrow.

"You shouldn't let her go," she said through a mouthful of food.

Surprise hit him harder than the enormous amount of calories he was consuming. "Why would you think—"

"I may be younger than you, but I'm not blind." She sopped up another bite of pancake on her fork and ran it through a river of syrup. "Anyone in three counties can see the way you two look at each other."

Apparently, Cora's brothers weren't the only ones who had clued in on his feelings for Cora. "Haley," he groaned. "It's not that simple."

"It is. You just don't see it that way yet."

"I've got a business back home, one I've worked hard to establish and maintain."

"I hear dogs grow just fine up here in Wyoming." She took a drink of her water.

"Again. It's not that simple."

She wiped her mouth with her napkin, and looked deep in his eyes. "Why not? If your contacts are drying up in Colorado, why can't you just move up here?"

"You think it's that easy to just up and move an entire business?"

"No." She quieted her voice. "But I think you have more people here than you realize who are willing to help you. Not just with moving your business, but with recovering from heart surgery."

Yeah, he hadn't figured out that heart-surgery part, either.

He stared at the heap of food in front of him. His appetite was suddenly gone, and he knew the meal was going to defeat him again.

Maybe this was about their past. Maybe her forgiveness couldn't cover the scars he left.

He set the bacon on his plate and wiped his hands with his napkin. "I know it's probably hard to hear I'm leaving again, but I'm not abandoning you this time."

She sighed. Then smiled. "Tripp, one thing that I've learned is that now that I'm adult, I can't be abandoned again. People come and they go. And that's okay. I have a community here in Elk Run that have become my family."

She reached across the table and placed her hand on his. "It's not the same. They aren't you, you could never be replaced. But they welcomed me with open arms when I showed up in this town and they're helping me get ready for this baby. I have a support system."

His little sister had grown up more than he'd realized.

And then Tripp saw it. Each step of Haley's life, she'd been taken care of by God. Each step of Cora's life, she'd been taken care of by God. Each step of his life, again, God had taken care of him. It wasn't that life was easy. It's that each one of them had been protected, guided, and held.

Which meant that from now on, God would still protect, guide, and hold them. Not *from* the pain of life. But *through* the pain of life.

"But if you really don't move here, I would love nothing more than if you'd visit and be my friend. Be this baby's uncle."

"I'm not missing out on my nephew's life. And I'm going to be here when he's born."

She withdrew her hand, placed it on her belly, and giggled. "You had a cardiac event at the last birth you were at."

"That's fair." He laughed, then he stared at his sister with affection. "You are going to be the best mom. And I can't wait to be around to see it."

Another jangle came from the front door and Tripp glanced up in time to see Cora enter with Hunter. Something kicked him in his gut.

"You're staring, Tripp," she teased. "Hunter's dropping her off so I can be her chauffeur for the day."

That used to be his job. His favorite part of the day. Another kick to the gut. Now he was headed back to Colorado to resume his normal business, something he had to keep reminding himself that he'd built from the ground up and loved. If he could remember his passion and commitment to his job back home, maybe leaving Cora wouldn't hurt so much.

Maybe.

* * *

Cora couldn't help but glance at the booth on the way into the diner. Her eyes were automatically drawn to Tripp.

He and his sister were tackling a Partridge in a Pear Tree. She had to hand it to him. He was nothing if not persistent.

Hunter led them to the vinyl seats at the bar and ordered himself a coffee and her a Coke. With the lack of sleep they'd all endured, she needed the sugar kick along with the caffeine, and she loved her brother for knowing that.

She propped herself on the stool, awkward with the boot, but was able to put her full weight on her leg. She was more than ready to give this boot the boot, so to speak. Only a few more days.

Why couldn't Tripp just stay five more days, until she got it off?

But it didn't matter. Even if he stayed, he'd still leave at the end of his four weeks like he'd originally planned. What difference would the additional five days make? That made her heart hurt.

"You're staring," Hunter said, facing the bar, a cup of coffee between his hands.

She turned and faced the same direction he did and huffed.

"You should just go talk to him."

Stacy placed a glass of Coke in front of her, winked, and walked away.

"I already did that. He's leaving. It's final."

"Nothing's final." He drew the coffee mug to his mouth and sipped.

"I can't change his mind, Hunter."

He shook his head as he looked at her. "Stubborn."

"I was raised by the best stubborn people I know." His

eyes narrowed at her, but she continued. "And I'm not talking about Mom and Dad."

"Mom and Dad raised you well. I just tried not to mess it up." He took another sip of coffee. "But I failed at that."

Was she hearing him correctly? "How can you say you failed?"

He set his coffee on the linoleum counter and turned his stool so he could face her. Indicating the scars on her face, he said, "I should have been there sooner. I should have been there sooner the other night, too."

"Is it your job to protect me from every kind of danger in life?"

He blinked. "Yes," he said firmly.

She smiled at him. "Hunter, if it's one thing I know, it's that no parent can protect their children from pain. Babies come out crying and the parents work their hardest the rest of their lives to soothe, love, and protect them. But they can't protect them from everything. It's part of growing up."

"It was my job to protect you."

She placed a hand on his arm. "If Mom and Dad had still been alive, I would still have gone out there and those wolves still would have attacked me." She gentled her voice. "Don't you see? It had to be you that was taking care of me that night. You acted fast and you saved me. God knew it had to be you. He chose you."

Something warred behind Hunter's eyes. She'd always worried about his high sense of responsibility. She wondered if her words cut the lies he'd told himself all these years down to size.

The tables had turned. This vulnerability from her brother was different. The confidence she had found in herself was new.

Her brothers had always seemed invincible to her, while she'd felt different. The scarred one. But Tripp looked at her like she could conquer the world. Every action she defined as a quirk, Tripp believed was part of her unique personality. What if she could believe that herself? What if she could grab hold of that kind of confidence and never let go?

But that kind of confidence didn't just come from Tripp.

What she'd come to understand was that God was always going to take care of her. It might not look anything like what she'd imagined. And it might not be pain-free. But He wouldn't leave her. He wouldn't forget her. He'd taken her scars and made them beautiful. Not just for Tripp, but for herself.

Tripp was right. She'd gone into the woods to help someone when she was seventeen. That's what she did. She helped people. And after all these years, she finally understood it to be full of beauty. Not of guilt.

Hunter turned to face the counter once more, picked up his coffee, and sipped again.

She smiled to herself. Her brother wasn't one for words. But that didn't mean he didn't feel anything.

She wrapped an arm around him and leaned on his shoulder. "You're everything I could want in a big brother."

"Does that mean you're going take my advice and ask Tripp to stay?"

She sent a death glare his way. It bounced right off his tall frame. "It certainly does not."

He shook his head. "I'm surrounded by idiots," he said with an affectionate tone and a smile on his face.

She couldn't help but smile back. Maybe someday her brother could find his own happiness. It felt like he'd found some peace from this conversation. She only wished he could also find peace with Ryder. Wherever their younger brother was.

"I don't want to interrupt," a familiar voice said from behind her, "but I'm headed home and just wanted to say goodbye."

Tripp.

Something ached in Cora's heart. She cleared her throat and pasted a smile on her face. When she turned around, she found Tripp standing there, with Rain at his side. Haley walked past them and stood in the front of the diner to chat with Stacy.

Hunter got off his stool. "Don't stay away too long," he said as he shook Tripp's hand.

"Let me know if you need any advice on setting things up with the therapy-dog program."

"Let me know if you change your mind about heading up the therapy-dog program."

Tripp smiled. "I appreciate it."

"I'm serious, Tripp. You change your mind at any point, just give us a call and we'll make room for you at Four Cross."

He looked down at the ground, then back to her brother. "Again. I appreciate it."

With a squeeze of her arm, Hunter slipped past her and mumbled, "I'll see you around."

Cora carefully slid off her stool. Favoring her booted foot, she carefully crouched down and stared at Rain. She took hold of her cheeks and pulled the furry face to hers. The beautiful dog looked back at her and seemed to be smiling. Cora chuckled and wrapped her arms around Rain. She whispered, "I think you healed something in me, Rain. And I'm so grateful to you." She pulled back and kissed Rain's head.

In return, Rain licked her cheek.

Cora's voice thickened. "Keep taking good care of Tripp."

When she looked up at Tripp, he held out his hand and helped her to stand, but didn't let go once she found her balance. He cleared his throat, and she noticed a sheen in his eyes.

"Don't get all emotional on me, Tripp."

"You can't bond with my dog, Cora, then ask me not to get emotional with you. Not after all you've been through." He bore his eyes into hers and, as he traced a gentle line down the scar on her cheek, whispered, "Not after all you've been through."

She squeezed his hand, not wanting to release it. Not wanting to let him go. "Thank you for helping me." She paused for a moment, unsure how to tell him what she was feeling. "And not just for driving me around."

The side of his mouth lifted in a half smile. "Your auto insurance company called to personally thank me."

She couldn't help but laugh.

This only encouraged him. "The mayor also reached out. He wanted to give me a key to the city because the citizens of Elk Run and the surrounding counties are so grateful I've been driving you around."

"That's not true," she said through a smile, trying to feign offense, but failing.

"It is. I got a pecan pie from the local Better Business Bureau and some home-grown vegetables from the farmers market down the road." He smiled wide. "Both with very specific thank-you notes about the roads I'm protecting with my service to the community."

Her shoulders shook with her laughter, which died down to giggles, then to a smile. But when the reality of the moment slowly hit her, the humor dissolved, and she fought back the tears that took its place. She looked down at the linoleum floor. "I hope you get everything fixed quickly so your business doesn't suffer."

What a stupid thing to say. But how could she say what she was really feeling? She couldn't ask him to stay—that wasn't fair to him. She shook her head. "That's not what I want to say. What I want to say is—"

He tugged on her hand and pulled her to him, then wrapped his arms around her. He leaned his head down and said softly in her ear, "I know." His heart pounded underneath her. Strong. Solid. "I know," he whispered again.

She held tight to him.

Rain leaned against their legs and let out a soft whine, as if she was sad she couldn't take care of both of them at the same time.

With one big exhale, he released her. When she pulled back, she saw the emotion swimming in his eyes.

"I'll see you when I come visit Haley," he said. "Take care of yourself, Cora. Ask for help every once in a while just so your brothers feel useful."

She stepped back and nodded. "Okay."

And just like that, Tripp took his dog and Cora's heart, and left the diner.

She was going to have to hold herself together. After all, she had a patient who needed her. But maybe today, instead of releasing tears after her appointment like her typical routine, she would let some of them out on the way *to* her appointment.

Chapter Thirteen

Five days later, under the sun of a crisp winter day, Cora stood outside the doctor's office and grinned at Hunter. She pointed her bootless foot onto the sidewalk and turned it one way and the other. "Good as new."

"Is it heavier?"

She cocked her head. "What? Why would my foot be heavier? I got the boot off."

"I don't know. But you can't afford to have your driving foot be any heavier than it was before the injury."

"Oh, come on," she said as she held out her fingers and wiggled them. "Hand me the keys. I'm not that bad. I only speed if I'm on my way to a delivery."

He held the keys high in the air so she couldn't reach them. "Are you forgetting that I was your guardian when you first got your license?"

"Stop worrying about me and hand me my keys."

He dropped the keyring in her hand and put his arm around her for a hug. "I'm your big brother. It's my job to worry about you."

She returned his hug, then stepped back.

"Ask for help once in a while. It makes the rest of us feel like we're useful to you."

"That's what Tripp said." After a moment, she looked at him and asked, "Um, have you heard from him?"

He crossed his arms over his chest. "Have you?"

She shook her head.

"Why are you so afraid to tell him how you feel?"

Her chest rose and fell as she released a huge sigh. "Tripp left, Hunter. Why would I put myself out there if he won't even entertain the thought of staying?"

"I'm sure he'll be back."

"Yes. When Haley gives birth." *Not for her.*

"If God can take care of you during two wolf attacks, can't He take care of your heart, too?"

She tried desperately not to take offense at her brother's blunt words. "Wow, you're not holding back this morning. Have you had too much coffee?"

"It's Chase who can't hold his coffee." Her brother always knew when it was time to steer the conversation to safer pastures. "Now that they've got a newborn, I'm worried that Chase'll be drinking even more java than usual."

She grinned. "I talked to him recently. He switches to decaf tea after his morning coffee. He says it tricks his tired brain into thinking he's drinking caffeine, but still lets him take catnaps when Noelle is sleeping."

Taking a few steps to the car, enjoying the bootless freedom, Cora said, "Speaking of babies, I'm off to meet a new patient. She wants to interview me and see if we're a good fit." She swung the car door open and hopped up in the seat. Then she pushed the button to move closer to the steering wheel. "Thanks again for dropping off my keys and SUV."

"Hope it goes well." He shut her car door and hit on the top of her car twice.

Cora drove away thinking about how light her foot felt

without the boot. And how heavy her heart felt without Tripp in her life. What if her brother was right? Maybe she should consider telling Tripp how she felt about him.

These were the kinds of the thoughts swirling in her head when she saw the red and blue flashing lights behind her.

"Oh, no," she murmured as she pulled over to the side of the highway and turned down the 90s hair band she had been singing with at the top of her lungs. She rummaged through her purse and found her driver's license, then popped her glove compartment open to retrieve her insurance card. Only on top of that card was a fresh package of Twizzlers she didn't remember buying.

Tripp. She couldn't ignore the longing in her heart. No doubt, he'd be laughing at her right about now, which caused her to smile.

In her rearview mirror, she could see the officer stride toward her with a baby face underneath his hat and a swagger that told her she might not be able to get out of this ticket.

She rolled down her window and smiled. "Hello, sir."

"Ma'am." He tipped his hat, the gesture polite, but doing nothing to hide his youth. Had he even graduated from high school? "Can I please see your license and insurance?"

"Absolutely," she said as she handed them over.

He promptly disappeared back to his car while she fidgeted in her seat. She stretched her right ankle, pointing her foot as far as she could, then flexing it back. Maybe the boot threw off her equilibrium in such a way that her right foot had been pressing a little too hard on the gas.

When he returned, he wore a stern face. "Can you please step out of the car?"

Shock bolted through her. "Is there a problem, Officer?"

"You have a concerning amount of warnings and infractions on your record."

"Oh, yes." She felt her face flush with heat. "I can explain. I'm a midwife, and I cover several counties."

He cocked his head. "I don't think your marital status has anything to do with this."

"No," she responded, tamping down a laugh. "No. I deliver babies. A midwife helps women through their pregnancy and labor. Out here in the country, where hospitals aren't as prevalent, I'm the one who shows up to help women deliver their babies."

He cocked his head, and his too-big-for-him hat slid just a little. "My momma had someone come to the house to help when she had my brothers and sisters."

"Is that so? Do you remember what her name was?"

"I don't have any idea."

She glanced at the officer's name tag on his uniform, but her hopes fell when she didn't recognize his last name.

"Well," she smiled, "that's what I do, Officer Warren. And sometimes I go over the speed limit a little like an ambulance would do getting to someone in need. Babies don't wait when they're ready to come into the world. If it would make you more comfortable, you can call Deputy Parsons and talk to him. He'll explain it all."

He raised his hat. "Deputy Parsons? Over in Elk County? He doesn't have any jurisdiction here."

Oh, dear. She must have passed the county line already. "I can assure you that what I'm telling you is true. Are you a new officer? I wonder if there's someone you could call to verify what I'm saying."

That was the wrong thing to say. At her mention of his being new at his job, Officer Warren's face turned to stone and he stood taller. All of the sudden, his age didn't matter one bit.

Stoic, he asked, "Were you headed to deliver a baby right now?"

Things just got worse. She couldn't lie about such a thing. She'd ruin her reputation. Plus, she could never live with herself if she used the precious babies she delivered to get her out of a speeding ticket. That felt like all kinds of wrong.

"Um, no, sir," she said, her tone not quite as cheery. "I was not headed to deliver a baby."

"Were you headed to an emergency of any kind?"

She bit the side of her lip. "Oh, well… No. I was not."

Fifteen minutes later, she was sitting on an uncomfortable bench.

In the county jail.

Tripp sped up the open Wyoming highway. Cora must be a bad influence on him.

He smiled. He'd like for her to continue to be a bad influence on him.

Something had changed.

Or maybe nothing had changed. He just wanted more.

He used to not want to wait to see her next steps. She intrigued him and surprised him each time he was around her. Now, he wanted to take those next steps *with* her. Doing life by her side, if she'd let him.

But first, he'd have to beg her forgiveness.

If he could find her.

He barreled up the Four Cross Ranch drive, then slowed down to the appropriate speed while taking the dirt road around the back of the property to Hunter's house.

He came to a gentle stop because he had precious cargo in the back.

Hunter came out on the porch before Tripp could get out of the car. He stood like a sentry cowboy with his arms crossed over his chest. "Are you lost?" he asked.

Tripp closed the driver-side door. "No. Do you know where Cora is?"

"Why would I tell you that?"

He looked down the road. Maybe he should have gone to Chase's house first. The new father might be too sleep-deprived to play protective big brother with Tripp.

When he looked back to Hunter, he said, "I think she'll want to hear what I have to say."

Hunter stood stock-still. "What are your intentions with my sister?"

He wanted to go there? Fine by Tripp. Man to man, he said with all confidence, "I'll let you know after I tell her. But my intentions are good."

Hunter's eyes darkened. "Do you have a job?"

"No."

"A place to live?"

"No."

Cora's brother shook his head. "Then what do you have?"

"I have her heart. And she has mine." He loved her. With everything in him.

A phone sounded, and Hunter pulled his cell out and glanced at the screen. When he answered, he softened his voice. "Hey." But after something the person on the other line said, his entire body locked. "What? Why would they lock you up?"

Hunter's gaze shifted to Tripp while he was talking, as if the call somehow applied to him.

When he finished the call, he slid the phone back into his pocket and stared at Tripp. "One question."

Tripp nodded, ready for the challenge.

"Are you sticking around?" Hunter asked.

"If she'll have me."

"Good," he said. "She may need you to drive her around again when they take away her license. But first, you'll have to bail her out of jail."

Jail? Tripp froze. "She got caught speeding again?"

"This time by a new officer in a neighboring county who doesn't know her."

He grimaced. "How was she?"

"Why do you think I'm letting you pick her up?"

"Right." Tripp motioned for Hunter to come to the back of his SUV. "Think you can take care of something for me while I'm gone?"

Approaching the now-opened back, Hunter asked, "Are you sure you want me to keep Rain when..."

His voice trailed off, and Tripp smiled. "They're cute, aren't they?"

Four German shepherd pups vied for the attention of the two men. Tails wagged, little pink tongues hung out, a few tiny barks emerged from the alpha puppy.

Behind them, Rain sat in her crate with her head resting on her front paws.

"What am I going to do with these little guys?" Hunter asked.

"We'll talk about that when I get back, if you're still interested in offering me a position to help out here."

"I'm still interested," he said, poking his finger through the crate and stroking one of the less active pups on the nose.

"Good." Tripp hefted the crate and walked it to his porch.

"Because I hired a guy to bring several other puppies along with all of my equipment to set up shop and help out here. But for now, can you watch these guys for a litte while? They've been cooped up, and I don't want them to have to wait while I bail out Cora."

"Story of my life," Hunter murmured, then looked to Tripp with a gleam in his eyes. "It's going to be fun watching you handle that."

Tripp hopped in his car, slammed the door, and shook his head. "Not as much fun as I'm going to have," he said while he looked over his shoulder and backed out.

Cora couldn't believe how this was playing out. The young officer who pulled her over had a sister who'd just given birth to her first baby, and the child was suffering from colic. It seemed Officer Warren was close to his sister, and on the way to the station, Cora had given him several tips to try to make things easier for both baby and momma. He'd definitely warmed up to her.

"Would you agree that I wasn't recklessly driving under the definition of Wyoming state law?" she asked from a bench behind bars. She certainly hoped he thought so. That was a misdemeanor waiting to happen.

"I agree, Miss Cross."

The receptionist poked her head in the room. "Miss Cross, a gentleman is here to see you. I'll send him back when he's done signing in."

She was prepared to placate whichever protective brother had come to get her. And though they were twins, she dealt with them very differently. "Which brother came? Was he a man of few words? Or did he look exhausted and cranky?"

"Neither."

Neither? That seemed odd to her.

Continuing to talk to Officer Warren about her speed infraction, she said, "I'm not sure you can accuse me of careless driving. I drive full of care for the person I'm visiting. That's why I'm trying to get there so fast."

The receptionist chimed in, "This one has a dog."

Cora forgot what she'd been saying to the deputy as excitement zipped down her spine. "A dog?" She heard the hope in her own voice. But it couldn't be. He'd left five days ago. She knew that for sure.

She stood, staring at the door, holding her breath while she waited.

Then Tripp strode through the door, wearing jeans and a navy Henley that brought out his piercing blue eyes, and stopped right in front of her. Rain stood at his side and seemed to also be holding back a smile, but she couldn't prevent her tail from wagging happily.

"Miss Cross," Officer Warren continued as if Tripp hadn't entered the room. "Caring for the people you're trying to drive to see doesn't justify the lack of care while actually driving."

This made Tripp grin. He stepped forward and wrapped his hands around the bars. With nothing but affection, he said, "It took you five days since I left to get arrested?"

"No." She walked to the front of the cell, and bent to greet Rain, who tried to push her nose between the bars to lick Cora. "I've only been behind the wheel for half an hour. It took me thirty minutes to get arrested."

Her heart beat wildly in her chest, and she stood to face him, placing her hands on the bars below his. She whispered the scariest question she could muster. "It took you five days to come back to me?"

"Sweetheart," he breathed, then placed his hands over hers.

That wasn't quite an answer. "Why are you here, Tripp?"

"I heard you might still need a chauffeur if they take your license away."

In the background, she could hear Officer Warren talking on the phone. "No, sir, Deputy Parsons. She wasn't belligerent. But at the academy, we discussed how careless drivers can become reckless drivers and I'm concerned Miss Cross appears to be such a candidate."

"Why are you here, Tripp?" she repeated.

"Because I work here now," he responded, edging closer.

"You do?" She angled closer to the bars.

He nodded, his eyes searing into hers. "My business didn't make sense in Colorado anymore. I got home and realized that the way everything so conveniently fell apart at the same time gave me the freedom to rebuild the way I want to. Where I want to."

"And you want to rebuild your business here?"

"No," he said.

She pulled back from the bars, but his grip on her hands tightened.

"I want to rebuild my business wherever you are," he said. "You might not always need my help, but I want to be by your side for whatever adventure you bring. I love you, Cora. I love your ridiculous candy habit and your unbelievable music playlists, and everything quirky and whimsical about you."

Tears stung her eyes. "Tripp," she whispered.

They both leaned their faces against the bars. "We make

sense together, you and I," he said right before he kissed her. Gently. Sweetly.

Rain butted up against Tripp, then licked her knee.

He pulled back just a bit. "We've got to break you out of here so I can give you a proper kiss."

"What about your surgery?" she asked softly.

He nodded. "I liked the doctor who helped me last week. I'm transferring my records to him so I can have the surgery here in Wyoming. We're thinking about doing it in a couple of weeks." He cleared his throat, looking a little unsure. "I wondered if you could help me out with that."

"I'll do anything I can for you, Tripp Blackburn." She swallowed. "You don't have to go through this alone."

"I'm starting to get that."

"Me, too." She offered a smile, hoping he could see the understanding, hope, and love. Because, yes, she loved Tripp.

"What are you thinking?" he asked.

"We do need to get out of here, but for a different reason. I actually need *your* help." When he cocked an eyebrow, she continued. "I need help with a baby."

He ran his thumb over her fingers. "That's your department, not mine."

She looked at him under her lashes. "It's a puppy."

His mouth gaped just a little and he looked at her in wonder. "You got a puppy?"

"I did," she said, smiling. "And I have no idea what I'm doing."

He lifted his hand and gently stroked down the side of her cheek, covering her scar with his palm. "My brave, brave girl."

"I love you, Tripp."

He pulled her in for another sweet kiss.

A loud noise sounded behind them, jarring Cora out of the moment. She looked to Tripp, covered her mouth with her fingertips, and laughed. His returning stare was packed with affection, and sparks of the future.

Officer Warren said, "You're getting off with a warning, Miss Cross. But only because Officer Parsons said I had to let you go immediately so you could deliver his next baby. Apparently his wife's in labor."

Tripp grinned at her. "Perfect."

"Perfect," she whispered.

Epilogue

Five months later, Cora leaned her head out of a hospital room door and flashed a smile to her annoyed brother.

"You're not going to make it on time," Hunter said, standing in the hallway wearing a suit.

"I am going to make it on time," Cora said, her head leaned out the door. "She's crowning and going to give birth any minute."

"Okay, then," her brother said, "Tripp's not going to make it on time."

"I'll make it on time," he called from around the corner.

"Tripp, honey. Haley's asking for you. Let's go."

Hunter held up a sheet while Tripp walked behind it and into the room, but not before Cora caught a glimpse of black tuxedo pants that poked out from underneath the hospital gown he had on.

"This is the craziest plan you've ever concocted. And that's saying something," Hunter muttered.

"Just hold up the sheet while Tripp walks by me and make sure he can't see me during the delivery."

"I can't believe you're delivering a baby in your wedding dress."

"I'm not delivering a baby in my wedding dress. I'm delivering a baby in scrubs. But it's our wedding day, and

Tripp can't see me before the ceremony. I'll hop into the wedding dress just as soon as we're done here. Then you can drive me to the church. But we'd make it there quicker if I drove."

"You're *not* driving," Hunter and Tripp both said.

When all was said and done, Haley gave birth to a precious baby boy, Tripp Wilder Seddington, named for her half brother and their mother's maiden name.

Haley made Lexi promise to take video of the Four Cross Ranch wedding. Lexi filmed while baby Noelle tried valiantly to teethe on her momma's phone during the ceremony. But not before Lexi caught the vows where Tripp promised to bail Cora out of jail for the rest of her life, and Cora promised to let Tripp teach their future children how to drive.

Rain made an appearance down the aisle, nudging her now little sister, a white Labrador named Snow. Tripp reached down to take the rings that were attached to the collars of each dog. But not before baby Noelle squealed and tried to launch herself at the puppy. Thankfully, Lexi had a good grip on her daughter.

After the ceremony, everyone walked through a buffet line in the ranch chow hall and filled their plates with all the fixings from dishes inspired by none other than the Elk Run Partridge in a Pear Tree. Fried chicken and waffle sliders, skillet potatoes, and a slab of ham were Cora's favorites. Plus, it was a guarantee that Tripp could finally claim that he had successfully eaten the culinary challenge. On a technicality, no less, but a victory for Tripp all the same.

Cora's three-tiered wedding cake stood elegant and whimsical, with various candies covering the entire bottom layer.

Tripp, quite dapper in his tuxedo if Cora did say so herself, twirled his wife on the makeshift dance floor. Cora felt beautiful in her sleeveless white gown. A layer of exquisite lace covered the entire dress. Underneath people could just about see her boots. Instead of a medical boot, though, this time she wore a pair of embroidered brown cowboy boots.

When she finished spinning, she laughed, leaned against him, and rested her head on his shoulder.

He kissed the top of her head. "Which playlist is this?"

"This is all the songs I listened to when you dropped me back at my house after our rides around town."

He pulled back, confused. "But these are all love songs."

"Yes." She grinned. "I think I fell a little bit more in love with you every time you drove me around the great state of Wyoming."

"Sweetheart," he whispered as he drew her in for a kiss.

A short kiss, because someone had approached them and cleared their throat to get their attention.

Tripp pulled back and rested his forehead on Cora's. "If this is one of your brothers interrupting another kiss, we're going to have words."

Cora giggled, then looked up.

"Ryder," she whispered. She released Tripp so she could throw her arms around her prodigal brother.

Upon contact, Ryder grunted and appeared to use one of his arms to shield his ribs.

She looked at him with concern. "What's wrong? Are you okay?"

He pulled her back in for a hug with his other arm. "Of course, I'm okay, sis." He held on longer than he'd ever held on to her before. "I'm so glad to see you."

His voice was full of emotion. She put some space between them, but didn't let go. His dark hair was too long, and his eyes held something weighty in them, something she'd never seen before. But his smile was genuine. He was a handsome man, even if he was her brother, in jeans, boots, and a starched, heavy canvas shirt. As dressy as the rodeo cowboy would ever allow himself to get.

She looked down and saw him holding a cane in his hand. What had happened to her baby brother on the rodeo circuit?

"I'm going to ask you again, Ryder Cross. Are you okay?"

"Nothing that won't heal," he said, flashing her one of his charming smiles. "Besides, that's not what's important right now. Congratulations, big sister." He reached a hand out to Tripp. "Congratulations, man. I'm—"

"Ryder!" Chase approached, baby Noelle on his hip, and pulled his brother into a one-armed hug. Ryder winced. "Wow. Look what the cows dragged in."

Ryder pointed at Noelle. "Look what you did."

"I believe I also had a part," Lexi said. "Hi, Ryder." She drew him in for a hug. "I'm Chase's wife, Lexi."

Ryder lifted his cowboy hat and nodded. "It's nice to meet you, Lexi."

Noelle took the opportunity to lean and reach for her uncle Ryder, who dropped his cane and cowboy hat and took her in his arms.

Cora rolled her eyes. "Ryder, you still get all the women to throw themselves at you."

He locked eyes with Noelle, just as entranced with the baby as she was with him. "You're beautiful, Little Bit."

She appeared pleased at his compliment, then promptly blew a raspberry at him and grinned.

He laughed as he passed her back to her daddy. "You've got your hands full there."

"Don't I know it," Chase said.

Just then, Hunter bent down, picked up the cane, and handed it back to Ryder.

No one moved or spoke while the two engaged in a stare-down.

And as if a decade hadn't passed, as if all the years of waiting for Ryder to come home didn't worry him, Hunter grabbed the back of Ryder's neck and pulled him into a long-overdue hug.

After a few moments, Hunter let him go, ducked his head, and stormed out of the chow hall.

Ryder's eyes were glued to the wake of his exit.

Cora sure hoped they could work things out.

Chase handed Noelle to Lexi, said something about checking on Hunter, and left the room. Noelle let out a whimper, and Lexi left, too, murmuring something about a diaper change.

Cora took Ryder's hand in hers and gave it a gentle shake. "You sticking around for long?"

He nodded. "Indefinitely."

She gave him a watery smile. "I'm so glad," she whispered. "Now, go get some food before we run out."

He winked and walked away.

Tripp slid his arms around Cora's waist. "You okay?"

"Yeah," she said. "Things might get interesting around here."

He grinned. "Who's next?"

"What do you mean?"

"Chase got married. Had a baby. We got married. Who's next? Hunter or Ryder?"

She laughed. "Between those two? There's no telling."

He snuggled her closer. "Maybe we'll just have to have a baby while we wait to see."

"Puppies, Tripp," she said, giggling. "Let's concentrate on all the puppies at the ranch first."

They'd just gotten a new litter of German shepherds and had their hands full.

As if Rain knew there was a family discussion going on, she sidled up to both of them and leaned in. Snow loped toward them, then skidded on the floor and bumped into Rain.

"Okay," Tripp said. "Puppies."

She nodded. "Puppies."

"And then babies."

And because she couldn't resist the thought, couldn't resist the man, she nodded again. "Then babies."

* * * * *

Dear Reader,

Thank you for letting me share Tripp and Cora's story with you. I hope their journey touches your heart as much as it did mine while putting it down on paper. And I hope that you smiled at Tripp's gaffe during their meet-cute, as well as Cora's candy-driven, heavy-footed driving.

The snowy isolation of Wyoming's backcountry and the warm sanctuary of Four Cross Ranch became the perfect setting for Cora and Tripp to confront their deepest fears. What happens when a woman terrified of dogs finds herself falling for a man whose heartbeat is monitored by one? Tripp's dog Rain becomes the bridge between them and leads them to healing. As it says in Hosea 6:3, "Then shall we know, if we follow on to know the Lord: his going forth is prepared as the morning; and he shall come unto us as the rain, as the latter and former rain unto the earth."

As hard as life's struggles may be for us in the moment, sometimes our greatest challenges give us profound blessings. Through Cora and Tripp's story, I wanted to show how God's healing works in unexpected ways, even through the very things that may have once terrified us. May His love rain down on each of you.

I am so grateful for you and I hope you enjoyed your visit to Four Cross Ranch. I'd love to connect with you at elizabethlongbooks.com where you can get updates about the Cross family.

Blessings,
Elizabeth

Get up to 4 Free Books!

We'll send you 2 free books from each series you try PLUS a free Mystery Gift.

FREE Value Over **$25**

Both the **Love Inspired®** and **Love Inspired® Suspense** series feature compelling novels filled with inspirational romance, faith, forgiveness and hope.

YES! Please send me 2 FREE novels from the Love Inspired or Love Inspired Suspense series and my FREE gift (gift is worth about $10 retail). After receiving them, if I don't wish to receive any more books, I can return the shipping statement marked "cancel." If I don't cancel, I will receive 6 brand-new Love Inspired Larger-Print books or Love Inspired Suspense Larger-Print books every month and be billed just $7.19 each in the U.S. or $7.99 each in Canada. That is a savings of 20% off the cover price. It's quite a bargain! Shipping and handling is just 50¢ per book in the U.S. and $1.25 per book in Canada.* I understand that accepting the 2 free books and gift places me under no obligation to buy anything. I can always return a shipment and cancel at any time by calling the number below. The free books and gift are mine to keep no matter what I decide.

Choose one: ☐ **Love Inspired**   ☐ **Love Inspired**   ☐ **Or Try Both!**
            Larger-Print   **Suspense**   (122/322 & 107/307 BPA G36Z)
            (122/322 BPA G36Y)   **Larger-Print**
                             (107/307 BPA G36Y)

Name (please print)

Address   Apt. #

City   State/Province   Zip/Postal Code

Email: Please check this box ☐ if you would like to receive newsletters and promotional emails from Harlequin Enterprises ULC and its affiliates. You can unsubscribe anytime.

Mail to the Harlequin Reader Service:
IN U.S.A.: P.O. Box 1341, Buffalo, NY 14240-8531
IN CANADA: P.O. Box 603, Fort Erie, Ontario L2A 5X3

Want to explore our other series or interested in ebooks? Visit www.ReaderService.com or call 1-800-873-8635.

---

*Terms and prices subject to change without notice. Prices do not include sales taxes, which will be charged (if applicable) based on your state or country of residence. Canadian residents will be charged applicable taxes. Offer not valid in Quebec. This offer is limited to one order per household. Books received may not be as shown. Not valid for current subscribers to the Love Inspired or Love Inspired Suspense series. All orders subject to approval. Credit or debit balances in a customer's account(s) may be offset by any other outstanding balance owed by or to the customer. Please allow 4 to 6 weeks for delivery. Offer available while quantities last.

Your Privacy—Your information is being collected by Harlequin Enterprises ULC, operating as Harlequin Reader Service. For a complete summary of the information we collect, how we use this information and to whom it is disclosed, please visit our privacy notice located at https://corporate. harlequin.com/privacy-notice. Notice to California Residents – Under California law, you have specific rights to control and access your data. For more information on these rights and how to exercise them, visit https://corporate.harlequin.com/california-privacy. For additional information for residents of other U.S. states that provide their residents with certain rights with respect to personal data, visit https://corporate.harlequin.com/ other-state-residents-privacy-rights/.

LIRLIS25

SNOWBOUND WITH HER PROTECTOR

ELIZABETH LONG

LOVE INSPIRED
INSPIRATIONAL ROMANCE

MIX
Paper | Supporting
responsible forestry
FSC® C021394
www.fsc.org

Recycling programs
for this product may
not exist in your area.

ISBN-13: 978-1-335-62136-8

Snowbound with Her Protector

Love Inspired
22 Adelaide St. West, 41st Floor
Toronto, Ontario M5H 4E3, Canada
www.LoveInspired.com

HarperCollins Publishers
Macken House, 39/40 Mayor Street Upper,
Dublin 1, D01 C9W8, Ireland
www.HarperCollins.com

Printed in Lithuania